I0673792

Richard H. Wilmer

Walter Martin

The factory, the school, and the camp

Richard H. Wilmer

Walter Martin
The factory, the school, and the camp

ISBN/EAN: 9783337391706

Printed in Europe, USA, Canada, Australia, Japan

Cover: Foto ©Andreas Hilbeck / pixelio.de

More available books at **www.hansebooks.com**

OR

The Factory, the School, and the Camp.

PUBLISHED BY THE

AMERICAN TRACT SOCIETY,

150 NASSAU-STREET, NEW YORK.

This narrative, truthful in its facts and simple in its style, is given to the boys and girls of our country by one who well knows the persons described, and who hopes their history may be an inducement to others to seek early the paths of peace and true wisdom.

CONTENTS.

6 CONTENTS.

CHAPTER X.

CHAPTER XI.

CHAPTER XII.

WALTER MARTIN.

CHAPTER I

THE WRESTLING.

DOWN the great stairs they went; down, down, one flight, two flights, three; men and women, boys and girls, with a few elderly faces mingled in the motley crowd; but the great throng principally composed of youthful forms. These went tripping along with buoyant steps, notwithstanding the labor they had been performing; for youth is elastic, and as they stepped out into the open air, and the fresh breeze fanned their cheeks, they laughed as gayly as though their work had been pastime instead of toil.

The bell of the large manufactory told them it was the hour for dinner, and here they were, the operatives of the Monimock Mills, where great webs of cotton sheetings were each day prepared for the market of the world. Two or three hundred women filed along, generally with the sweet freshness of youth shining out under their simple cape-bonnets or dilapidated straws, with shawls of every conceivable texture and hue, and dresses of chintz or delaine, soiled or clean, tattered or whole, according to the characteristics of the wearers. Men were there too, in greasy overalls, with slouched caps; or neat and tidy, because the unsightly overdress had been left hanging in the mill, while they went home in a clean suit with a manly air.

How refreshing was the pure air. How glad was each one to escape the noisy workhouse. And yet, labor there was more agreeable than in some situations. Many a merry laugh echoed within those walls; many a lifetime friendship was formed and cemented there.

But if a few characters of noble mould were there, it must be acknowledged that the main current of thought was low. The coarse jest, the rough words, and the worthless song all furnished proof of the uneducated and unsanctified state of the hearts within. To a person who reflected that each soul here was destined to live for ever, when earth and its transient pleasures have passed away, it was painful to witness the great want of serious thought, or of desire to prepare for the last great change.

There was one wish common to all who toiled here, and that was, to receive the wages of their labor, the money due for continued diligence. For this they all wrought, the young and the old; for this they spent their breath, and shut themselves up with the scent of the oil and the click of flying wheels.

Not that all used their money with discretion, for some wasted it as snow wastes before a noonday sun; but all wanted it. For it children were placed here; children who ought to have been in school were obliged to work their daily round, compelled by avaricious fathers or poverty-bound mothers, or because they were orphans, and must earn their own living in the world.

Down they come now, a band by themselves, shouting, tumbling, tripping and jostling each other about with the wildness and abandon of the untrained spirits of headstrong boys who had been curbed for five hours, and now were liberated for a brief season of freedom. Like young colts loosened from the stall, and permitted to caper and frisk in the green fields, these boys caught the freshness of the open air, and indulged the impulsiveness of their untamed natures.

"I say, Jim, come on," shouted Tom Hardy; "let's have a rouser. Come out here, and pitch into me, if you want to. I'll show you how quick I'll lay you flat."

"That's right; go it, boys," said Ned Manson; "any thing for fun. Stand back here, boys; give 'em fair play. Now take him, Jim. You can beat him any time."

"Beat me!" said Tom, drawing himself up to his utmost height; "I should like to see the boy that can do that."

"Hurrah then; I'm the one," said Jim, laying his hand upon the shoulder of Tom. Quick as thought they grasped each other, and began manœuvring with efforts to put each other on the ground; while the other boys grouped around, cheering and shouting as the game went on. For the moment, dinner was forgotten.

James Clark, or "Jim," as he was called, was a delicate, slender boy, the son of a pious father, and it seemed a pity that so good a man should expose his son to such influences for the sake of gain. Better remain at home, even with privations, than risk the temptations of dangerous associations.

Tom Hardy was strong and burly; and if he lacked the agility of Jim, he compensated for it by sturdy strength and firmness of compact limb. He had a fancy for trials of strength, and always rejoiced when his rough challenges were accepted. Jim, with his sanguine temperament, agility, and suppleness, was not willing to yield the palm, and so the present contest became warmer than they intended.

"Hurrah!" cried Ned Manson, as one

or the other seemed likely to fall; "bet you a treat Jim will beat him."

"Nonsense," cried another, "Jim a'n't half so stout as Tom. I'll take your bet. Tom 'll beat."

Thus the youthful contestants and the youthful spectators were already sharing those high excitements which, followed into manhood, lead to the race, to cards, to high betting, and then to the treat, the flushed cheek, and the unsteady hand.

At this moment another boy came down the stairs, and stepped quickly upon the threshold of the open outer door. He was a thoughtful-looking youth of thirteen, with a keen black eye, and a pleasant, but resolute countenance. He paused suddenly at the sight of the now almost angry wrestlers, and gazed upon them with a look of surprise.

"Take care there," said Ned, who seemed to be chief speaker; "take care,

Jim; keep cool, or Tom will have you.
See, Walter," turning to the new-comer,
" do n't they handle each other well ?"

But Walter did not reply. He still
stood on the threshold, with an expression of mingled pity, contempt, and dis-
gust.

Poor Jim was growing tired. He had
thrown his whole energies into the first
efforts, with a determination to break
down the big, blustering Tom; but now
he was exhausted, and Tom, taking a
sudden advantage, laid him flat upon his
back, and then gave a shout of triumph.

The boys scattered at once; there was
no more time to lose, and Tom, giving a
glance of triumph at his fallen adversary,
started upon a run like the others.

Walter Martin, however, remained
watching the defeated Jim; and seeing
that he needed help, went to him and
helping him to rise, brushed the dirt from

his clothes, smoothed his hair with his own pocket-comb, and then walked by his side.

"How came you in such a scrape?" said Walter; "I should n't think you would meddle with such a fellow as Tom Hardy."

"Well, he dared me," said Jim, "and the boys would all laugh if I backed out, and say I was a coward."

"I should let them laugh then," said Walter.

"I suppose you would," replied Jim; "you can do different from anybody else."

"Why can I do different?"

"Oh, because you do n't care if the boys do laugh at you."

"Yes, I do care," said Walter; "I do not like to be laughed at; but if they tell me I am a coward because I will not fight, I think it requires more courage to resist the accusation and persevere in the right than it does to fight, and so I think I have more true courage than they."

"Yes," said Jim, "I know you have. You never fear to face the boys at any time, no matter what they are doing; but I can't do as you can."

"Why not?" said Walter.

"Why, the boys would laugh at me."

"Yes, there is the trouble," said Walter. "You fear the laugh, and so you fight. Try now, and see if you cannot show moral courage, the true courage that faces evil and conquers it; and if you cannot at first resist the boys, keep away from them."

"But how can· I keep away from them."

"Do as I do. ·Wait a little when the bell rings, and do n't get into the rush. Stay behind, take off your overalls, wash your face, comb your hair, and brush your clothes, then you can go home looking like a gentleman. Then do n't go back a minute too soon, so that the boys can't have time to tempt you; and by and by you will like my way much better than your old way. Besides, what would your father say if he saw you where I did?"

By this time they had reached Jim's door, and he went into the house, pondering Walter's last question, "What would your father say?" His father did not live in the village, but three miles out, on a small farm. He was a good man, but as his farm furnished him little money, he sent his son to the factory to earn more, not thinking that possibly this might lead to vice and ruin. But God, who "seeth not as man seeth," had a watchful care over the son of the honest, praying parent.

Jim ate his dinner silently, still considering Walter's advice and his last

question. Then putting on his cap, he
waited at the door till he saw Walter
coming back, when with a bright smile
he ran out to meet him.

"Walter," said he, "may I go and
come with you, so that the boys need not
laugh at me?"

"Yes," said Walter, "I should be glad
to have you."

"Thank you," replied Jim. "I have
been thinking of the question you asked
me, and I want to quit the company of
those rude boys; for I know my father
would feel bad if he thought I was doing
wrong. I should not like to have him
know how I behaved this noon."

The bell had ceased its working call,
the men and boys were in their places,
the long, steady mules were just recom-
mencing their patient roll, back and forth,
back and forth, bearing as they went
their long rows of spools, from which the

fine cotton threads spun out their even length, twisting, whirling, buzzing, and sometimes snapping, requiring the agile movements of nimble fingers to join them again and keep the machine in running order.

The overseer had just hung up his coat and stepped out into the room as Walter and James entered, so the boys had but little chance to begin any sport with the discomfited wrestler. They could only wink, twist their faces into meaning grimaces, cough with a peculiar sound, and extend such sly hints to him as they were sure he would understand. He went quietly to his work, taking no notice of these manifestations, and the room assumed its customary activities.

The boys who assisted the spinners were called "back boys," because it was their duty to go back of the mules, and taking away the spools which had been

emptied of the cotton roping, replace
them with full ones, from which to spin
the fine threads. They also assisted in
keeping the machinery clean, and were
general waiters for the men who employed them, each man having a boy assigned him.

Sometimes the boys took a cloth, and
while the heavy machine rolled its way
forward to the spools, they stooped to the
floor on the other side, and rubbing the
cloth on the straight beam, slipped rapidly through underneath the low rails,
coming out safely on the other side before
the machine rolled back, with a force
which would have crushed the luckless
one who had been caught lagging. A
spectator, unaccustomed to the sight,
would have shuddered for the fate of the
boy, who himself had no fear.

Tom Hardy having a great desire to
know the mind of Jim, dusted his mule,

filled his spools, and seeing that every thing was right, took a trip across the room, "to see if Jim was sore," he said.

"I say," said he, coming up to him; "do you feel good after it? If you do n't, I 'll give you a little more to-night; just for fun, you know."

"Halloo, here," said Walter, who had seen Tom's movement, and followed him; "do you see the old man there, Tom?"

Tom looked around, and saw the man for whom he worked, and whom he usually designated as "the old man," in a towering passion. He was a man of an imperious temper, and not pleased to have his "back boy" running off without leave; so without stopping for more words, Tom made haste back again to his work, receiving a kick for leaving, besides knowing that the boys were all laughing at his discomfiture. There was no more trouble for Jim that day.

CHAPTER II.

STUDYING AND IMPROVING.

NIGHT came, suspending the day's labors, and again the bell jingled its welcome summons; welcome always when it was a release from toil, but sometimes greeted with a sigh when it called back the half-rested ones to a renewal of their duties.

"Wait a little, James," said Walter; "let the crowd go. I have something here for you."

So James loitered behind, and then he and Walter preparing themselves tidily, followed the other operatives down the broad stairs.

"I have a book here," said Walter when they were out in the street; "sometimes I get a little time to read in the mill, and if you would like it you can have it this evening. You may be lonely if you stay at home, and I hope you will not go out. If the boys are to have a high time, let them have it without you."

James accepted the book, gave the requisite promise, and Walter ran for his home. It was always a pleasure for him to get home. The sight of his dear mother's face, the evening reunion of the family circle, the well-spread board, the books, the papers, the few minutes' private consultation concerning the next day's family arrangements, all these home scenes were dear to the loving boy.

The youngest of a band of six brothers, delicate, thoughtful, and domestic in his habits, it was not strange that Walter was the pet of his mother, and was regarded generally as the household baby. Some of his older brothers worked in other departments of the same mill; and though in their own private circle they sometimes jested the young boy too roughly, they were very careful that others should not do so. So his elder brother Frank, finding that Walter must go into the mill, and that this was his father's firm decision, went to the overseer and exerted his influence to procure him a situation under an honest, sober man, who treated him always with consideration and kindness.

It was well for Walter that he was thus protected. It is a wise saying, that "God tempers the wind to the shorn lamb;" and in this case the great Father was not unmindful of the fragile lad, but threw around him the arm of his protection.

Books were Walter's unceasing companions. He carried them to the mill, he sat up late to read them, he walked

the streets with them in his hands, and
he even carried them to the table with
him; though the laugh of his larger
brothers, and the name of "bookworm,"
prevented the repetition of the last act
as often as he would have liked.

He did not read trashy novels, but a
well-selected assortment of histories and
biographies, even ascending the scale to
a few scientific works and an occasional
poem. Deprived of the benefits of school,
and shut up to the routine of daily labor,
he yet contrived to keep pace with those
of more abundant privileges, and his
countenance assumed the intelligent expression of the young scholar, instead of
the vacancy of the mere drudge.

"I never see that boy," said one gentleman to another as Walter passed them
on his way to the mill, "but I think
he will not always plod in this factory
path."

"He is a fine-looking boy, certainly," replied the other.

"He is more than fine-looking," continued the first speaker. "His fine looks are the result of noble thoughts; it is not mere physical beauty he possesses. Studious, truthful, diligent, respectful, he bids fair to become one of our best and truest men."

Thus the good conduct of boys is observed by men oftener than boys think; their characters, good or ill, become stamped in the eyes of the world as well as in their hearts and countenances. Indolence and vice leave sure marks on the countenance and demeanor, as well as intelligence and virtue.

That factory bell, how punctually came its notes through the still morning air, pealing on the ears of all who followed its behests. Some started slowly, and with many groans and yawns, being jaded out with late hours and dissipation, and not refreshed by slumber. It was otherwise with Walter and his brothers.

"A person feels paid for early rising such a morning as this," said Walter, gazing upon the gorgeous clouds of the eastern sky. "Come, let us hurry, Nat, and take a run down the bank before the second bell rings. We shall feel the better for it."

"Agreed," replied Nat, who was two years older than Walter; and speeding down the back stairs, they were going out at the back door, when they met their mother.

"Why, mother," said Walter, "I believe you are always up; I can't get up first if I try."

"Why shouldn't I get up?" she replied; "my children are obliged to get up, and it is right that I should."

"Oh no, mother; we are young, it

does not hurt us to see the early dew,
but you ought to rest."

"I could not rest if you were up," said
she; "it is my happiness to share the labors of my boys," laying her hands upon
the heads of the two. "Long may I be
spared to rise in the morning and care
for you, my industrious, faithful sons."

How the touch of her gentle hand, and
her kind words, strengthened their young
hearts, as bounding down the bank, they
took a run by the side of the swiftly flow-
ing river, coming out by a circuitous path
near the mill. Here they found flocks of
women, men, and boys hurrying to their
daily toil.

Our two boys placed their hands upon
the rails of the fence separating the
meadow-path from the street, and with a
brisk leap came over into the road, just
as Tom Hardy and his band came out
from their boarding-house doors.

"Hallo, Nat!" said Tom, "why didn't you come down to Conant's last night? Had a high time down there, I tell you."

"Had something else to do," replied Nat drily. .

"Wonder what?" said Tom. "Cooped up with Walter, under mamma's apron strings?"

"Couldn't stop for that," replied Nat, "hurried to bed so as to get up in season this morning to wash the bed-feathers off my face."

Tom's anger flashed, as involuntarily putting his hand to his forehead, he rubbed thence some of the down which had clung to it from his landlady's leaky pillow. But it was useless being angry with Nat. He was proverbial for his coolness; and his dry sarcasms, cut where they might, or hit as they would, were commonly endured by the boys without retaliation.

James waited till he saw Walter and Nat, and then joining them, went quietly along in their company. Nat worked in the card-room, so Walter and James entered their own room together, as they did the day before.

"Hurrah!" said Ned Manson, "I believe Jim has got under Walter's wing. Poor fellow; got so whipped yesterday, he is afraid to go alone. Halloo, Jim; have you tied yourself to Walter with a bed-cord?"

How Jim burned at the taunt; but a wink from Walter prevented his reply, and the starting of the machinery precluded further conversation.

Walter was never very happy in the mill. He longed for more time to read, more time to study and to think; he wanted different associates, companions whose thoughts sometimes soared above the spindle and the loom; for he looked upon life as a gift too sacred to be trifled away in thoughtless jests or light amusements, or bartered for sensual enjoyments. Something in the boy looked upward, and though his hands were tied to daily toil, his brain was busy with flying thoughts, and his heart was every day learning lessons of patience and love.

In his eagerness for knowledge, he often laid upon the window-sill near his work his open book—grammar, history, algebra, or geometry—and as he flitted back and forth at his labor of dusting, removing spools, carrying boxes, or mending the frail, snapping threads, he would pause for a moment at his window, read a sentence in his book, and then revolve it in his mind as he darted back to his work.

He was so faithful, diligent, good-tempered, and obliging, that he was a great favorite with his master, who carefully avoided harshness or unkindness in deal-

ing with him.   The other boys regarded
his situation with envy, and thought all
the men were partial to him on account
of his brother Frank, who was the second
overseer of the room and a general favorite.

It was true, Frank had used his influence in the selection of Walter's master;
but beyond that, the good conduct of the
boy himself had won all the kind treat-
ment he received.   This was a point the
other boys overlooked.   They did not
consider that their own "shirking," care-
lessness, and ill-temper, brought upon
them the kicks and abusive language so
frequently and plentifully showered upon
them by the impulsive men who employed
them.

But Walter's kindness to James had
awakened new feelings in the heart of the
wayward boy, and he watched his kind
friend with a lively interest.   He wanted

to know how he found time to read and
study so much, without neglecting his
work; and he was surprised to see how
diligent and quick he was in performing
his work, how every thing seemed to be
done beforehand, never lagging, never
out of the way when wanted.

"I don't wonder 'boss Abbot' is kind
to him," soliloquized James. "There isn't
a bit of chance to find fault. I wonder
how it would operate if I should try his
way. I might as well try it, any way.
It isn't very pleasant to have my ears
boxed and my hair pulled just when
'boss' has a fancy;" and brushing back
his hair with his hand, he flew about
with such a bright smile and buoyant
step, kept up the threads so nicely, and
polished every thing so beautifully without being asked, that "boss Wyman"
looked on with amazement.

" What's got into the boy?" thought

he; "it is perfectly surprising. Some remarkable fit has seized him. I did n't know he could do so much."

"That's firstrate, Jim," said he; "you have made the old machine look like new. You can rest ten minutes, if you want to. There's nothing to do now."

It was James' turn to be astonished.

"Boss Wyman, of his own accord, tell a fellow he may rest! I did n't know there was a streak of kindness in him. That's because I tried to please him. I wonder if the other boys would n't succeed as well, if they should try. I'll run over to Walter's window, and see what that book is."

The book proved to be an elementary work on natural sciences, and was open at a page on the laws of light.

"Do you read such books as this?" asked James. "I thought they were such as are studied at school."

"So they are," replied Walter; "but you know I cannot go to school, and have to study as I can."

"But what's the use?" said James; "it isn't of any use for us to be great scholars, and trudge around the old mill all our days. If we learn ever so much, nobody will know it."

"But," replied Walter, "we need not stay here all our days, if we can know enough to do any thing else. Or even if we stay, we shall be more respected, and become overseers or something else."

"But we do not need to be extra scholars to be overseers," replied James.

"The more we know, the better overseers we should be; or we could go into the counting-room, and keep books; or at least we can have the pleasure of knowing, and of being respectable men. But how came you over here? Boss Wyman will scold you when you go back."

"No," replied James; "he gave me ten minutes. I had done up the work so close there was nothing to do. I tell you, I begin to think it's better to pattern after you than after Tom Hardy and Ned Manson. But I must go back now;" and James returned to his work with a smile on his face and a smile in his heart.

"Wake up here, Tom," said Tom's master. "Don't you see the roping is all out there? Fetch on some boxes here, or I'll make you tingle."

Tom started suddenly. Burly as he was, he dared not disobey these sharp-toned orders, though his head ached from the last night's dissipation, and he felt much more like sleeping than he did like bringing heavy boxes of roping.

The ringing of the bell once more sent all hands home from their work; and Ned and Tom dropped their occupations,

and ran as rapidly as possible. Walter
and James followed behind, as usual.

"Let's wait a little," said Ned; "I'm
going to get Nat to give us a treat to-
night."

The boys paused at the card-room
door to wait for Nat, and as he came
out, Ned caught him by the shoulder.

"Halloo here, Nat," said he, "you are
just the fellow we want. Go down to
Conant's with us to-night."

"Start along there, boys," said a voice
behind, and Nat's brother Frank stepped
down the stairs. "Go home to your
dinner, and be back in season."

Frank was their second overseer, and
the crestfallen boys were obliged to obey.

CHAPTER III.

THE MORAL FAMILY.

In Mr. Martin's family, morality, a strict observance of the proprieties of society, and honorable, fair dealing with all men, were accounted among the first duties of life. Never were six boys more thoroughly instructed in the portion of the commandments relating to the duties of man to man than they.

Profanity in all its multiplied forms was strictly forbidden, and the smallest child would have been punished for the utterance of a profane or vulgar word, or for any substitute for swearing so commonly adopted by those whose consciences will not venture really to take the name of the great God in vain.

Lying was as strenuously prohibited,

and "the truth, and nothing but the truth," was the motto for the youthful band, enforced by parental authority and parental example.

Temperance too was a ruling feature. Mr. Martin himself was a devotee in the cause of temperance. He lived it, and he talked it. In temperance meetings his voice was often heard; and not a boy of his, from Frank down to Walter, ever dared to sip a drop. Their evenings were especially guarded against this temptation, and they were required either to remain at home or give a reasonable excuse for absence. They did not want strong drink, because they had not learned to love it, or to like the class of boys who frequented the haunts of dissipation.

Every boy must be in at an early hour; not in a barren home, devoid of interesting pursuits, but in a home where books, periodicals, newspapers, and music fur-

nished abundant occupation for leisure
hours. So the boys grew up intelligent,
virtuous, and respected.

But here the father's influence paused.
Having inculcated this outward morality,
he seemed strangely to forget the higher
commands. The first and greatest, "Thou
shalt love the Lord thy God," was forgotten in the mind of the worldly man.
The love of Jesus, faith in his name, the
beauty of his life, the necessity for a
change of heart, eternity, and the great
unknown future, all were subjects unmen-
tioned in family conversation.

How blind is the human heart; how
forgetful of the requirements of Him who
has made the world and all that is in it!

There were two sisters mingled with
this band of brothers, to give freshness
and life to its evening gatherings. It
was a happy family; but with the exception of the elder sister, the requirements

of religion had as yet met with no response. She alone had learned to pray, and to draw sweet waters from the fountain of Jesus' love.

Under these circumstances, there was one point of true morality which occupied a doubtful position in the family regulations. The observance of the Sabbath stood on a poise; it might be well kept or it might not, as circumstances occurred.

"Don't go to church to-day, Ellen," said Frank one Sabbath morning as they were at breakfast. "I borrowed a copy of those new poems last night, and I want to read them to you to-day."

"Cannot you read them after I come home?" asked Ellen. "You know I do not like to be absent from my place in church. Come now, go to church with me, and then you can read to me when we come home."

"I think it will storm before noon, Ellen," said Mrs. Martin; "perhaps you had better not go to-day."

"A little storm wont hurt me, mother; I can dress for it, and take my umbrella. Come, Frank, go with me," said Ellen pleadingly; for she loved her brother, and she loved the house of God, the sound of prayer, and the faithful pastor's words.

Frank looked out at the window, pondered a minute, and then replied, "I don't feel like it to-day. What is the use for me to go there, when I want to read this book? I shall not have much time to read this week, and I wanted to read to you to-day."

Poor Ellen; she was a young Christian, loving Christ in the depths of her heart, but not very well fortified with reasons for the observance of the Sabbath, except that she knew God had commanded it. She had none at home to teach her the way of life; and though the Spirit of God, like a little lamp, threw light upon the dim chambers of her soul, she offered to compromise with her brother, and join him in reading the poems, if he would first accompany her to church. She did not yet realize that every hour of the day is holy to God, but was firm in her determination to go to church.

"Who will go with me?" she asked, looking around the group. But the younger boys were all imitators of Frank, and pleaded other occupations.

"I don't see any use in going to meeting," said the rattling Herbert. "People that go to meeting are no better than those who stay at home. Now there is Ned Manson, as wicked a fellow as there is in the mill, but people say his father is a church-member. And there is Wheeler, who prays in the evening meetings and is terribly pious every Sunday, and yet he will cheat every man he trades with."

"That is the way it is," replied Mr. Martin. "Professors are no better than other people, nor ministers either. The best way is to do about right, avoid every thing bad, and we shall come out well enough. 'Pure religion and undefiled before God is, to visit the fatherless and widows in their affliction.'"

"And to keep yourself unspotted from the world," added Ellen.

"Yes," said her father; "that is, to do right, and keep yourself from bad company and bad deeds, which I hope my boys will ever do."

The explanation fell far short of Ellen's ideas of the meaning of the word "unspotted." She pondered it as she walked alone to the house of God. "Unspotted. Perfectly pure. If we gaze at a sheet of new-fallen snow, how dazzling and white it appears. The unspotted heart must be just so pure; and it cannot be so, unless we live very near to God, and have our hearts washed in Christ's blood."

But Ellen found little courage to express her thoughts at home. She met with so many antagonisms, so many arguments, and so much reliance on good works, or "living about right" as they expressed it, that it was a wonder she kept within herself so much of the light of faith as was found there. Ah, Christ was true to his promise; and while Satan threw water on the fire to quench its light, the loving Saviour drew near, and secretly fed it with the burning oil of his grace. So he ever does to those who trust in him. Glorious Saviour, holy is thy name.

Walter had been an attentive listener to the morning's conversation. In the mind of the young boy there was a restless longing, a seeking for something which he had not. There was an upward looking of the soul, which he himself did not understand. He plunged into his studies and his reading, but was not satisfied. The book which alone could satisfy him was yet unread.

True, there was a large Bible on a shelf by itself in the library; but he had seldom seen it read, except by his mother on a Sabbath-day. There were other Bibles in the house, and he knew that Ellen always had a pocket-Bible with her; but it had never entered his mind that this book contained the secrets of the heavenly and true wisdom, and was a balm to the weary soul, a refreshing to the thirsty heart.

Ellen could have pointed him to this book, but she had no thought that he was seeking for the pearl of great price. There was so strong an opposition to real religion among her brothers, that she did not speak of the subject to them; and she lived among them without thinking that in their minds there might be a restlessness which mere morality could not satisfy.

The breakfast being finished, and the house still, Walter wandered around for somebody to talk with. Frank was stretched on the sofa, absorbed in his poem, Mr. Martin and the boys were scattered about reading, and Ellen was at church. At last Walter found his mother in the kitchen, sitting quietly alone, with the large Bible on her lap.

This was just what he wanted. He thought his mother must be a Christian; he was sure she could not live such a beautiful life, unless she had something in her heart to guide her footsteps; yet she had never spoken to him on this subject.

"Mother," said Walter, "what makes

Ellen so particular to go to meeting every Sabbath?"

"Because she enjoys going, and she thinks it is right to go," replied his mother.

"Well, mother, you seem to like to go sometimes; but you are not so particular about it. If it storms, or any thing occurs to prevent, you stay at home. But Ellen will not stay for any thing. She would not even stay to please Frank this morning. Was that right, mother?"

"I think it was," replied his mother. "It certainly is right to sustain the worship of God. We are all dependent on Him; he is the great Author of all things, and it is right that people should serve and honor him."

Never before had Mrs. Martin said so much as this; but the inquiring expression of her child had drawn out her thoughts surprisingly.

" Then I am sure," said Walter, " we are very far from doing right. There is not one in the house, except Ellen, that ever feels the least responsibility about going to church. Father and all the boys think it quite a burden to go, unless some remarkable man is going to preach, or some special topic is to be introduced. Temperance meetings, lyceums, political meetings, and all such gatherings they attend if it does storm."

Mrs. Martin was puzzled. She hardly knew what to say. Her own example had not been perfect in this respect, and her conscience was too busy to permit a ready reply. But she was relieved from her difficulty by the merry sounds of feet and tongues coming down the back stairs, eagei to pop corn at the kitchen fire.

The corn was popped and eaten, and the whole family were still collected in the kitchen when Ellen came in from church. The sight touched her heart painfully. They were all tidily dressed, and seemed vieing with each other in kindness; but Ellen remembered it was the Sabbath, and she wished that her brothers loved the house of God, and her father too. If he would only go to church oftener, what an influence it would have. Then there was the Sabbath-school entirely neglected, and Ellen almost doubted whether they were truly a moral family. "Is it really morality," thought she, "to neglect the church, and break the fourth commandment by doing our own pleasure on God's holy day?"

Walter had, for the time, forgotten the brief conversation he had held with his mother that morning; but Mrs. Martin well remembered it. Why should Walter ask such questions? She dwelt much on the matter, revolving it in her mind while she prepared the dinner.

The keeping of the Sabbath was indeed a test-point in the family. She knew many families whose heads were professors of religion, that had no family altar, and in that respect she thought they were no better than their family. But those. people went to church, at least when it was pleasant, while her boys did not like to attend church at all. And when it was pleasant, they sometimes walked out, either in the street or rambling in the fields; arguing that as they had so little time for breathing the fresh air during the week, it was necessary for their health to use the Sabbath for this purpose.

At her suggestion, Walter went to church with Ellen in the afternoon. Frank continued reading his poems; Mr. Martin tried an afternoon nap; the boys found something to read, and the Sabbath wore away, leaving its record to be reviewed at the final day.

CHAPTER IV.

THE CONVERSION.

Months passed on, leaving little trace of their footsteps in the band under Mr. Martin's roof. All were still there, treading the usual round, save the second son James, who had gone to the Saranac wilderness of New York. He was missed from the group, but frequent letters told of his prosperity, and already some of the brothers were expressing a desire to follow him. Mrs. Martin was glad they did not want to go farther west; she could not spare them for that, for her sons were her hope and her joy.

Walter still went daily to the mill, and there too were Tom and Ned and James.

A bright but cold day had come, and Walter's overcoat was buttoned to his chin, as he ran back to his work after dinner. James, as usual, came out to join him.

" Walter," said he, " I have heard there are to be special meetings down in the lower church. They commence to-day. Don't you want to go?"

"I don't know," said Walter, "we don't have time."

" We can go in the evening," replied James. "I want to go down to-night, and I wish you would go with me."

" Well, perhaps I will."

In the mill, Walter found the meetings were the general topic of conversation. Large numbers of the men expressed their determination to go; and so did many of the boys, laughing and jesting however, as they told their various reasons for going.

"I wish you would call for me this evening," said James, as he and Walter left the mill at night. "I had rather go to the meeting with you than anybody. You saved me from becoming like those boys, and have been my protector and friend; and I want you to teach me the way to heaven."

"The way to heaven!"

Walter repeated the expression to himself as he walked slowly home. "The way to heaven! Why, I do n't know the way myself. How can I teach him? What made him say that to me?"

Then Walter recollected how pale James had recently looked, how thin and delicate he was; and he thought, "Well, perhaps he will go to heaven by and by; who knows? I 'll call for him to-night, certainly."

The evening was clear and beautiful, and the church was already crowded when Walter and James entered; so passing up the aisle, they took some low seats near the pulpit, just as the minister rose in his place to invoke the divine blessing on the services.

The Rev. Mr. Jones, the preacher that evening, had enlisted under the gospel banner from love to Christ and a deep sense of the worth of souls. His preaching had been attended with signal success, and the more he labored in this sacred work the more he loved it. Winning souls to Christ became his chief delight, and this evening he commenced his sermon with, "Behold the Lamb of God, which taketh away the sin of the world."

How closely he portrayed to the heart its depth of guilt before God, its wicked unbelief and rejection of the offers of pardon, and its utterly lost condition. Then came the proclamation of Jesus, the propitiation for our sins, who took away our guilt, and cleansed us with his own blood. The congregation melted under the fervor of his words, and eyes unused to weep shed tears that night.

Walter had heard impressive sermons before, but never one that moved him like this. Every sentence was fraught with meaning to his awakened sensibilities. He saw his heart in a new light, and the blackness of its guilt opened to his consciousness. No longer did he feel himself removed by good works from the vilest sinners who lived. Conviction followed conviction with deeper thrust, and he went home with the barbed arrow deep within him. James was sad and depressed; but so absorbed was Walter in himself, that he scarcely noticed his companion at all. He wanted to do something for his own salvation; but coming to Jesus, believing on him alone, seemed so simple, that his self-righteousness could not understand it.

Surely there must be something for him to do somewhere.

That night he found a Bible and read long before he retired; but everywhere he found threatenings and condemnation. True he read, "Come unto me, and I will give you rest;" "He that believeth shall be saved;" and, "Him that cometh unto me I will in no wise cast out;" but his excited mind seized hold upon none of these promises. He did not think they were for him. Everywhere was doubt and gloom.

The next morning he went to his work as usual, but there was no peace in his heart. He did not speak of his feelings, and none knew the struggles and conflicts with which he was contending.

James too was occupied with his own thoughts, and though sure that Walter was under deep conviction like himself, he dared not mention it.

"I wish I dared speak to him," said he to himself; "I want to tell him that we ought to love Jesus—that I think that would make us happy, and would fill that unsatisfied longing he sometimes talks about. But he does not look at me to-day. I do n't know what to think of him."

Neither of the boys said much about the meeting; but in the evening, when Walter went again, he stopped before James' door and found him ready.

Again the preacher presented Christ, for Christ was his favorite theme; and deeper yet went the sure arrows of conviction which accompanied his words. The house was pressed to its utmost capacity, and the preacher seemed to sway the hearts before him as the heart of one man. Could any steel themselves against such searching appeals? He drew himself down to his audience as though he was one of them; could any resist?

The third night found Walter and James again there; and this time, when a request was made that those who desired prayers should signify it, James was the first to go. Walter was surprised. In all his anxiety he had not thought of doing that; it would be so public. No, he was going to God by himself; or if he perished, he would perish alone.

But James' bold step startled him, and he began to consider what he should do. That night the young soul of James drank of the waters which his Saviour gave him. He had yielded. He laid himself at the foot of the cross, he accepted Christ for his salvation, and henceforth his trust was in Him. The next morning he waited for Walter as usual, and the light of joy beamed in his eye as he met him. All fear of him was gone, for the Saviour's love had taken away the fear of man.

"Walter," said he, "I am so happy."
Walter started as if stung by some pierc-
ing thought.

"Happy, happy!" the very words
jarred upon Walter's ear. What was
happiness? There was certainly no such
thing for him, and he did not reply.

· "Walter," continued James, "I have
found Jesus. My heart is so light, and
I have such joy. Do n't you want to find
him too?"

Walter looked at him earnestly a moment, and then replied, "Yes, James, I
want to find him, but I can't; I know
not where he is."

"Why, he is everywhere. His love
fills every place. You have only to say,
'Here, Lord, I give myself to thee,' and
you can find him at once."

What a sudden change passed through
the soul of the stiff-necked boy. The ice
was broken, he had spoken his thoughts,

and now his pride broke down, and he poured the feelings of his heart into the ears of his young friend.

"You must pray." said James.

"I do pray, but it does no good."

"Oh, it will do good. God will hear you; he always hears. You must ask for the prayers of Christians to-night."

"Oh, I can't do that. The boys at home will laugh at me. They think there is no need of going to church."

"I thought you did n't care for people, if they do laugh."

Alas for Walter; he knew not what to say. He who had walked with such a fearless air, feared to show himself among those who prayed. The boaster had fallen, he had acknowledged himself afraid.

"Where is Ellen?" said James. "Why do n't she go to these meetings?"

"She is out of town this winter. She is teaching."

"If she was at home she could help you now, and tell you what to do."

"Yes," said Walter, "perhaps I should have told her before this. She would understand me."

"Well, go to meeting with me to-night; let the world know that you seek Jesus, and he will come to you just as he has come to me. He will fill you with joy and peace; you will see his glory, and we'll praise him together, both here and hereafter."

James had taken Walter's hand with a firm grasp, and looked earnestly in his face, till he promised that he would come out publicly that evening, as an inquirer for the true and living way.

He did so, and as Christians pleaded in his behalf at the throne of grace his heart throbbed. He felt as though bound with a thousand chains; his pulse quickened, and he said to himself, "I will yield. I

will give myself to Christ." Then his
will came up again in all its obstinacy,
and said, "You can't; where is the use
in trying? Besides, how do you know,
after all, that there really is any Jesus
who hears you? Perhaps it is all a
farce?"

. Near him stood an elderly Christian
woman, who had noticed the changes of
his countenance, and turning to him, she
gave him such a look as caused every
nerve of his body to thrill.

"I never saw such a look," said he
afterwards to a friend; "a look of pain,
of anxiety for me, of yearning love; a
look as from eternity. It revealed to me
the day of judgment; it flashed into my
soul a crucified Saviour, and exhibited
my sin in disobeying him. I saw that
she at least believed without a doubt, and
my own doubts instantly fled. Should I
rebel against God? Could I endure his

wrath if I did? No. 'Blessed Jesus,' I said, 'take me now. Save me; I rebel no longer. I am thine. Henceforth I am thine, forever thine.'"

"Oh, Walter," said James, as they were walking home, "I knew when you became a Christian."

"How did you know?" asked Walter.

"By the light of your eye and the happiness shown in your face. Let us bless God together. Come in to my room before you go home, and let us thank God together."

And there the two new-born souls first knelt together to praise Him who loved them and bought them with his blood. How sweet are such praises in heaven. We know they are heard there, for does not the word of God say, "There is joy in heaven over one sinner that repenteth?"

The next morning Walter and James

were at their places as usual, but a new light shone in their faces, and they had prayed that it might shine in their lives. Many of the mill hands had attended the meetings, and a close watch had been kept over all who seemed interested. It was soon known that James and Walter were among those hopefully converted, and significant looks and whispers passed around among their old acquaintances, David Nealy, Tom Hardy, Ned Manson, and the rest. They too had attended the meetings, and been somewhat impressed by the services; but at their close each evening they had gone to their usual resort, Conant's, and dissipated whatever feeling they had, amid strong drink, cigars, and profanity. Already they were learning to love the fatal cup, and to take a glass; while the fumes of strong drink and tobacco were their especial delight. How fearful in

the last great day will be the woe pro-
nounced on the men whose vicious example and ridicule of religion closed the
eyes and hearts of these youth while the
Saviour was passing by.

CHAPTER V.

THE LAST FAREWELL.

THAT was a happy winter for the youthful converts. Many besides Walter and James had passed from death unto life. The voice of prayer and hymns of praise were heard in many rooms, the meetings were full of young worshippers, and all through the mill were scattered joyful hearts, triumphing in Christ's love.

Walter no longer regarded the boys with the pride he had formerly manifested; he spoke to them kindly, and sometimes walked with them, conversing so pleasantly that the hearts of some began to warm towards him. Unconsciously the oath and the rough jest were suppressed in his presence, and he tried to induce them to join the Sabbath-

school. Thus he honored his Master even
among those who could not understand
the change, and who yet discerned the
power of Christ in their young companion. Happy are those, young or old,
who live so near their Saviour that he is
reflected in all their conduct and honored
by their daily life.

When the spring came, with its chill-
ing winds, Walter noticed that James
did not seem so strong as usual. There
was a flush on his cheek, a short breath,
and a frequent cough that increased daily.

"James," said Walter one morning,
"I don't think you ought to work; I
don't believe you are able."

"I do feel weak," replied James; "but
you know I have to pay my board, and
if I don't keep busy, I shall fall behind;
and I don't like to send word to father;
he cannot afford to keep me at home
long."

"Well, come up and stay with me a week. Mother will be glad to have you, I know, and she will cure you."

"I should like to," said James, "if the overseer is willing."

Walter made haste home, and in a few minutes was back again with his mother's consent. All was readily arranged at his boarding-house and at the factory, where all pitied the gentle and patient James, and were ready to divide his work among them.

That same forenoon James was welcomed to Mrs. Martin's hospitable and motherly care. Lizzie brought pillows and a warm spread for the sofa; and as he stretched himself upon the soft couch he gratefully said, "This is so comfortable, I shall get well soon, I am sure."

Walter, at his mother's request, bought some slippery-elm to carry home at noon. He had great faith in his mother's medical powers. "She is better than a doctor," he used to say.

"But your mother can't save him," said boss Wyman, "nor the doctors either. I have known this good while, that he was going to die. He is a good boy, and I hate to spare him. When he first came here he did n't do very well, but this religion of his brought him right round."

"So you see," said Walter, "religion is a good thing. Sometimes you think it is worse than nothing."

"Oh, the true, genuine religion is a good thing, I suppose; but I do n't think much of this 'cant,' that is all talk and no practice."

"That is n't religion," replied Walter.

"Folks think it is," said Wyman, "and they 'll pray, and pretend to be very good, when they are no better than I am, and do n't try half as hard to do right as I do."

"Trying to do 'about right' never can save us," said Walter; "Jesus Christ saves us. He died for our sins, and we must believe on him as our Saviour, and love and serve him."

"Oh, I do n't know any thing about that," replied Wyman; "somehow I can't understand it; but I am glad James does, for when a person is going to die, I suppose it's a good thing."

"Yes," said Walter, "and it is a good thing to live by too. It will make you happy every day."

Walter was saddened at the thought that his friend was going to die, but he rejoiced that the beauty of his every-day life had borne testimony to the truth as it is in Jesus; and he knew that this same loving Jesus was in heaven, and would surely receive one who loved him so well.

"It is only passing through the valley

a little sooner than I do, that is all,"
thought he. "I shall follow him when
my work is done. May I be as ready to
go as he is."

Three days passed, when Mrs. Martin
said they had better send for James'
father. His father came, and the best
efforts were made for his restoration;
but still he faded, and at length he was
wrapped in overcoats and blankets, and
kindly carried home.

"Have you heard from Jim to-day?"
said Tom Hardy to Walter, a fortnight
later.

"Yes," replied Walter, "I saw the
doctor this morning. He thinks he is
failing, and will not live many weeks. I
shall go out Saturday night, and stay all
night with him."

"I wish I could go," said Tom. "May
I go with you, Walter?"

"Yes," said Walter, "I should be

glad to have you. We will buy some
oranges and such things, and carry
out."

So the reckless Tom took the Saturday
night, which was generally spent at the
tavern, for visiting the sick young Christian. It proved a blessed Saturday night
to the wayward youth.

James was glad to see them, and extended his thin hand as cordially to Tom
as to Walter, though a look of surprise
passed over his face when he saw him.

James was very feeble, so that it was
necessary some one should sit up with
him through the night. Walter immediately offered his services.

"No," said Tom, "you stay to-morrow, and sit up with him to-morrow
night. I must go back in the morning,
and I will take care of him to-night."
Then recollecting himself, he added,
"Perhaps you think I can't take care

of you well, I am so rough. But I can, and I will. I will be gentle as a lamb."

The two friends looked at each other for a moment, and James replied, "I should be glad to have you, if you are willing."

When all had retired, and they were left alone, Tom felt awkwardly. He smoothed down the pillow and arranged the clothes, but still did not speak. The truth is, he had come all the way out there to confess to James, and to ask his forgiveness, but he did not know how to begin. James spoke first.

"Tom," said he, "the doctor says I must die, and I feel it too."

Tom's firmness gave way, and tears fell from his eyes as he grasped the wan hand. "I know it," said he; "will you, can you forgive me?"

"Forgive you!" said James; "for what?"

'For treating you so, ever since we had that fight."

"That fight," said James; "why, I was just as much to blame as you. How wicked I was."

"Not so bad as I was," replied Tom. "And how many times I have laughed at you since about your religion."

"That was only because you did not understand such things. Let me ask you now to become a Christian, and give up your wicked ways."

Then followed a long talk, at the close of which James gave Tom his Bible, and Tom promised to read it faithfully.

A month passed by, and James was yet alive. Every day his faith grew stronger, and the light from his dying-bed was aiding to accomplish that which the meetings had begun; it was working a revolution among the men and boys of the spinning-room. Some of them visited

him, carrying their little tokens of good-
will, and receiving in return his testimony of the sweet peace which he found
in the Redeemer, and earnest entreaties
to seek his love.

His serene state of mind was a general
topic of conversation among his friends;
and when evening came, Tom and Ned
were no longer seen at the tavern. They
began to think they too must some time
die, and they wanted to be prepared.
Frank Martin too, often spent the hours
of the night by the side of the happy
sufferer, each time getting a clearer view
of the realities of another world.

The last day came at length, and the
loving spirit was gently released, and
returned to God who gave it, and to the
Saviour who redeemed it.

CHAPTER VI.

FROM THE MILL TO THE SCHOOL.

SURELY and steadily the leaven of reform was working among the band of boys in the spinning-room. The effect of the glorious departure of the young Christian lingered like the departing twilight of a radiant summer's evening. The boys were more faithful at their work; the men became more lenient; there was less profanity, less kicking, and less scolding.

Tom's reformation had produced a wonderful influence. When he commenced reading his Bible, and threw the weight of his strong will on the side which Walter defended, there was a general surprise; but though his old intimates sneered at him, and though his

love for liquors and cigars strongly tempt-
ed him, he firmly resisted every foe, both
inward and outward, read the treasured
Bible, the gift of the departed, and faithfully kept the promise made in the still
hours of that long-remembered night.
Ned and David too gradually changed,
under the strong influence of Tom and
his urgent appeals.

Thus a year escaped into the past.
Walter had grown to be quite a tall boy,
and had been promoted from back-boy
to become himself a spinner, in charge of
a mule. And then came other changes,
to Walter agreeable, and important in
their results.

There was a depression in the times,
mercantile houses failing, money hard to
be obtained, and the manufacturing company decided to suppress a part of their
works. A portion of the mill was to re
main unused, and consequently many of

the operatives must be dismissed from employment.

"I suppose," said Mr. Fiske to Frank Martin one morning, "that we shall stop about half the mules in our room, and one or two in the lower spinning-room. It is hard to say who must leave; the men will hardly know how to find employ-ment, and I dislike to say who shall go."

"I heard Walter say he hoped you would send him away," replied Frank.

"Ah, why does he want to go?"

"He wants to go to school; and he says father will never be willing as long as he can have work to do here. Father likes to see us all earning."

"Very well," said Mr. Fiske, "let Walter be one to go then."

Presently Harry Martin came running up the stairs from the lower spinning-room, where he had so quietly-worked hitherto.

"Mr. Fiske," said he, "I understand there is to be a mule stopped in our room."

"Yes," said Mr. Fiske, "I suppose there must be."

"Well, I have come up to ask you if I might be the one excused?"

"Why, I have just excused Walter. Do you want to go to school too?"

"No, sir, I want to go to New York, where my brother is. I have wanted to go for a long time, and this is just the season to suit me. Up in the Saranac region where he is, there is plenty of game, and splendid fish, and big forests. He is taking deer now all the time, and I must go."

"Very well then," said Mr. Fiske; "you are a prime workman, Harry, and I should like to keep you; but it is better to send away those who want to go than those who do not, so you can go."

Mr. Martin was in great consternation

when it was announced to him at the dinner-table that Walter and Harry had. both left the mill.

"I don't know how we shall get along," said he, "if you all do so. Times are hard, and you can't find so profitable employment anywhere else."

"I don't want employment," said Walter, "I want to go to school; and the old mill is in trouble. I am glad I can get away. If the work had not stopped I should never have dared to ask to be excused."

"If you go to school a while," said Mr. Martin, "what then?"

"I do not know what then," replied Walter; "we will see if I know any thing first."

"I think he had better go to school," said his mother; "he has wanted to go for a long time."

"Well," replied Mr. Martin, "I suppose he must then. But what are you going to do, Harry?"

"Why, sir, I think I'll go up to the Saranac region. They are bagging the game there, and sending it down the Hudson rapidly."

"Oh, Harry," said his father, "it is bad enough to have one son off there in the woods. I do n't want another there. I want my boys to stay with me."

"I do n't know but he had better go," said Mrs. Martin. "I have many anxious days and nights about our lonely one there, and if Harry is with him they can be company for each other, and take care of each other if they are sick."

Mr. Martin yielded; and then Nat, who was almost eighteen, put in his plea for a few months' visit to the Saranac with his brother. This too was allowed, and only Frank and Herbert were left to follow the routine of the mill.

Walter felt like a new being. The burden of an uncongenial mode of labor was removed from his shoulders, and his spirits rebounded with an elasticity he had never felt before. He collected his books together, and kneeling in his chamber, thanked God for opening to him this opportunity of improving his mind, and prayed that he might have grace and strength to improve it aright, and might become an honor to his Saviour and a blessing to the world.

Walter hardly knew where to place himself, or what rank he could take in school. His studies had always been so much by himself, that he felt a diffidence about comparing himself with those of more favored opportunities. He expected to be far behind them, but determined to exert himself and keep as near them as possible.

He was agreeably surprised therefore

when the teacher, after a brief examination, assigned him to the first English
class in his school. He feared Mr. Train
was mistaken, and had placed him too
high.

"I have never been in school much,
sir," said he; "I am afraid that is too high
for me."

"You have studied by yourself, you
told me."

"Yes, sir," said Walter, "I have had
no teacher."

"But you have been a thorough student. In whatever branch I have ques-
tioned you, I find you have a perfect un-
derstanding. I should advise you to
commence on Latin. You have not
studied the language, you say?"

"If you please, sir," said Walter, "I
should prefer a term under you in the
common ·branches first. I should like
your instructions in English grammar,

and such branches as are pursued in district schools. If I can become fitted for it, I should like to teach."

"As you please," said Mr. Train. "I have no doubt but you are as well fitted to teach now as half our teachers; and half of the other half," he added, smiling.

Walter seized upon his studies with avidity. As the parched earth absorbs the falling rain, his thirsty mind drank in the instructions of his teacher.

"I never saw any thing like it," remarked he; "if he should teach with the same avidity that he studies, he would be the best teacher in town."

This remark was made in the hearing of a gentleman who, a few days after, was in a district three miles out from the village where they were wanting a teacher.

"Our means are not large," observed Mr. Brown, one of the committee; "we cannot afford the highest price for one of

the first •teachers, and yet we want a
good one."

The gentleman told him of the remark
which Mr. Train had made with regard
to Walter Martin.

"Walter Martin," replied Mr. Brown;
"I know him very well. He is a fine
little fellow, but I did n't know he was
qualified to teach."

"It seems he has qualified himself,"
replied the gentleman. "Mr. Train
places him in the front rank of his English scholars, and is anxious he should
have a school, to prevent his going back
into the mill."

"I tell you, wife," said Mr. Brown,
"he is just the one for us. He can board
in our family. I 'll ride out and see him
this evening. Don't you want to go and
call upon Mrs. Martin?"

"Yes, I have been wishing all day
that you would invite me to ride."

That evening the agreement was completed, and Walter was so moderate in his price, that it was found they could have four months of school, which sent Mr. Brown home in high spirits. He lost no time in communicating to his neighbors the rare bargain he had made, and the long school they would have; being careful to add that he boarded the teacher a little under price, which would also help to lengthen the term.

Walter sought his pillow that evening with new feelings in his heart. He had wanted a school, but now that it had come he almost shrank from the undertaking.

"I am so young," he thought, "will the scholars fear and respect me?"

Then he remembered the Saviour who had so often been his refuge, and kneeling before him he thanked him for giving him this school, and prayed for assist-

ance and a blessing in the discharge of
its duties.

The fall term of the academy closed
the week previous to the annual Thanksgiving. Nat had just returned from his
Saranac tour, and Ellen came home, so
that all but two gathered round the
Thanksgiving board.

The Monday after Thanksgiving, Walter entered upon his new scene of labor.
Mr. and Mrs. Brown gave him a cordial
welcome, and in the school-room he was
greeted with smiling eyes from the youth
of the district, who were already in their
seats, awaiting him. He opened the
school with prayer, and soon found himself quite at ease.

He had his own ideas of teaching, de-
rived perhaps from studying so much
by himself. He determined that whatever he taught should be thoroughly
taught, and he threw into his school so

much zeal and earnestness of purpose, that the scholars, catching his spirit, studied and learned as they had never done before.

"You are doing wonders in our school," said a farmer to him one day. "My children never learned so before. What do you do to them?"

"Come in some day, and see," replied Walter.

"I will," said he, pleased with the invitation; and soon the scholars were surprised to see the farmer and his wife walk into the school. The invitation was extended to others so cordially that they could not refuse; and one after another, the staid farmers found their way to the school, where everybody was so wide awake. The fame of these things reached the village.

"You are succeeding finely, I hear," said Mr. Train, as Walter called upon him one Saturday evening. " How is it you do it?"

"I hardly know, myself," replied Walter, "except that I feel so much interested in my school, that I interest my pupils. I have tried to teach them self-respect, and that it is of the utmost importance that they not only learn their lessons, but learn them thoroughly; and that they strive to become useful in the world, and to be noble men and women, remembering that they are accountable to God."

" You have struck the right chord," said Mr. Train ; "it is far better than scolding and whipping. May God give you grace to persevere."

" Thank you," replied Walter. " I called to ask you to lend me your physiological charts; I have promised my first class some lectures on physiology."

"Certainly," said Mr. Train, "I am happy to lend them."

Walter thanked him, and hastened home to his mother.

"Mother," said he, "are not the weeks long without me?"

"They would be, my son, only I know you are happy in your occupation; and what is your happiness is mine. I hear that you are succeeding finely," said she, "and I am very happy to know it."

"I have tried to do well, mother. God opened the way for me, and I ought to do all I can."

At the annual town-meeting, a brief notice of each school was usually read in presence of the assembled voters of the town. Walter was anxious to know what was said of his school, and he crowded in among the men, that he might distinctly understand the reader.

He found that his school was ranked as the second in town.

"Only one teacher better than I am, and he an experienced teacher," said Walter to his mother, in reporting to her what he had heard. "Now I can easily get a school another winter."

"I am very glad," she replied, "both for your sake and my own."

CHAPTER VII.

THE CHASTENING.

WALTER had now earned enough to keep him at the academy until another winter, and the consent of his father and mother was easily obtained to this plan. Both were pleased with his success, and were anxious he should have all the advantages they could secure for him. His teacher, and others who had become interested in him, advised him to prepare for a college course.

He was in doubt respecting this plan. It seemed to him a great undertaking, with no available resources except winter teaching. He must have clothes and books; even his preparatory studies could not be completed in his own village, and if he went away there would

be the expenses of his board in addition.
He could not see how he could even prepare for college, or how go through it if
he was prepared.   .

Mr. Train advised him not to look forward so far as that, but to commence,
and God would open a way for him in
his providence.   He accordingly entered upon the study of Latin and the
higher mathematics, and so continued
through the season, until another winter
approached.

There was another subject upon which
he had not yet decided, and which troub-
led his mind with a continual anxiety.
He had not yet made a public profession
of religion.   He was anxious to form an
opinion upon the respective merits of
the several denominations; and he read
various authors, examined articles of
faith, and studied inquiringly into the
differences which separated the many

churches. But the more he examined, the more puzzled he became. The pastor upon whose ministrations he attended, conversed with him on the subject. He advised him to put away every theological book but one, and that the Bible. "Read that," said he, "and that alone. It is simple in all the ideas necessary for our lives here, and presents the great truths fresh from the Creator. Above all, pray. Pray for enlightening wisdom, pray for the Holy Spirit, which will guide you into all truth."

Walter followed his pastor's advice; and God, who saw his struggles, led him into paths of light and peace.

In another part of the town there was a small but beautiful village, containing a school-house, a few dwellings, one or two stores, and a church. The citizens went to the main village to vote; and here in town-meeting they had listened to the annual report of the schools, and the high commendation of young Walter, and it was agreed among them to seek his services for the ensuing winter in their school. It was an excellent situation, much superior to the one he had occupied the previous year; the offer of it was pleasing to him, and was at once accepted.

There were yet three months before the school was to open, and the earnest student renewed his zeal and study, giving special attention to algebra, geometry, and trigonometry. Meantime he loved the house of God, interested himself in the Sabbath-school, and had a ready word of kindness and counsel for every one in trouble; but like the weary dove, he as yet found no rest for the sole of his foot in the church of Christ. He wanted a home with the people of God; but where?

In the midst of these occupations he was brought to a sudden pause. In the chamber of feverish agony lay his darling brother Frank, the first-born of the sons.

Every heart was hushed, and every labor suspended, while the band of brothers united in care for the sick. But the fearful day came, the last day, and the twilight of an autumnal eve threw its dreary shadows into the room, where, amid the assembled family and friends, the sufferer lay, with his head upon his mother's shoulder. The eyes of the dying young man glowed with unwonted brightness, when, meeting the gaze of his brother Nat, he said,

"Nat, this is a hard spot, the hardest in which a man can be." Then looking wistfully up to his mother, she replied with the words,

"Jesus can make a dying bed
Feel soft as downy pillows are,
While on his breast I lean my head,
And breathe my life out sweetly there."

He bowed his head in assent to the truth of the precious verse, and was gone, for ever gone.

There was sadness in the hearts of the stricken family. This was the first death in the cemented circle. After-breakages might follow, but they would touch a fractured ring, tremulous with the lingering vibrations of the first shock.

The young teacher returned to his school with new views of life. Death had come very near to him, and at its call he renewedly consecrated himself to God, praying for grace to live the good man's life, that he might die the good man's death.

He found in his school plenty of labor to occupy his time, and break up any lethargy which might steal over him. There were a large number of pupils, many of them quite advanced in their studies; and he was obliged to be active and industrious, that they might be properly instructed in the variety of branches pursued. Thus he was compelled to banish the inertia consequent upon his late bereavement, and resume the elasticity so necessary to success.

"The selection of my boarding-place must have been by a higher power," he remarked to a friend visiting his school, "for my especial benefit. My host is 'a host in himself,' and I find myself strengthening and improving daily under his care. He is just the guide I needed."

"You must be spending a pleasant winter then," replied his friend, "for I see your school is very agreeable. I am glad of your success."

When Walter returned to tea, his welcome was cordial. Mr. Childs, who was the pastor, had completed his preparation for the next Sabbath, and was just in the mood for an evening's chat.

"So, you have finished another day's work," he remarked, as Walter entered the sitting-room. "So have I. I have been pressing on to-day, to be ready for the Sabbath; and I think this evening you and I will spend with the ladies."

"Thank you," said Walter; "I shall be happy to do so."

"Yes; I knew you would. It is not well for you to shut yourself up in your room all these evenings, poring over your books. It will make you morbid; and a man with 'the blues' cannot live as a Christian should."

"I see," said Walter, "you do not believe in a dull and gloomy Christianity."

"Indeed I do not," replied he warmly.

"Christ did not come into the world to make us desponding and sad. He came to make us happy; and how can we be happy unless we are cheerful? When we realize the bounties of our heavenly Father's bestowing in this life, and consider that beyond it we have the promise of eternal life, how can we be otherwise than joyful? I think you told me you learned to love Jesus long ago, but have not yet united yourself to his church."

"Yes, sir," replied Walter, "that is the case. There are some points which I am unable to decide, and I'm waiting to see more clearly."

"Don't wait too long for that, my young friend. You must not stay out in the cold, freezing your heart for the want of Christian sympathy. Decide upon something, and get where you can feel at home. It will do you good. As a man is happier for a loving home in this world, so a Christian is happier to have a loving home in the bosom of Christ's church. It is the command of our Saviour. One of his last acts was the institution of the Lord's supper; and he who neglects this, neglects one of his greatest earthly privileges."

"I am aware of it," replied Walter; "but there are conflicting views held by the different churches, between which I am unable to decide."

"This is probably the result of your early education," said Mr. Childs. "Not having been accustomed to attend a church regularly in your early days, you have not learned to love one more than another. But I hear the tea-bell. The ladies are expecting us, and after tea we will have some music."

Mr. Childs led the way to the tea-table, followed by the young teacher; and as his genial smile shed its lustre over the bountiful board, and his voice invoked the blessing of the Most High upon the food before them, Walter felt how beautiful were the Christian virtues, when displayed in the every-day duties of life.

"Besides claiming you for this evening," said Mr. Childs as he filled Walter's plate, "I must speak for you to-morrow, as I believe you have no school. I want to take you round among the people."

"Thank you," said Walter; "but I suppose my mother will expect me home to-morrow."

"Ah, well, you ought to go home, to be sure, for your mother's sake. But we'll make a few calls first, and then Willie shall take the pony and drive you out home, if you please."

Walter accepted the proposal, and found his heart growing warm and cheerful, in social contact with the generous, open-hearted, hospitable home scenes by which he was surrounded.

"Now, Ada," said Mr. Childs to his daughter, "we hope you will furnish us some music. Our young friend here will supply the tenor, Miss Abigail," nodding to the sister of his wife, "will give the soprano, and I think I can add a little bass."

The piano was rich in its tones, the music selected of a choice character, and Walter enjoyed an hour or two of mingled conversation and music with a keen zest.

"These evenings are my recreation," said Mr. Childs. "They give me a pleasant relief when I am wearied with the labors of my calling."

Thus the wise pastor sought to dispel the morbid gloom of the young teacher, and to prepare him for a candid and healthful examination of the truths which he did not fail carefully to inculcate.

Before spring Walter had united himself to the visible church of Christ; and soon found, in his growing love for the people of his choice, that minor differences of opinion vanished before the warm sun of Christ's love.

At the next annual town-meeting, Walter had the happiness of hearing his school ranked first on the list.

"I am truly thankful for your success," said his mother, when he had repeated to her the encomiums bestowed upon his school by the committee. "It is from the same wise source from which comes down every good and perfect gift."

CHAPTER VIII.

PROGRESS.

WALTER seemed now to be fairly on the course he had so long desired to traverse. He had been successful in teaching, and his heart warmed with love for the work.

"There can be no higher privilege," he said, "than to lead young immortal minds in the ways of knowledge and virtue. They love to learn; all children love to learn, if the instructions are made interesting to them. If the teacher is earnest and zealous, the pupils catch the spirit, and will follow wherever they are led."

The pastor of his church urged upon him the importance of preparing for the ministry; but he could not feel confident that he had a call to the work.

"It is a noble, a holy work," said he, "but I cannot feel sure that God has called me to it. Indeed I do not yet see clearly to what he has called me. I have succeeded as a teacher. I love the business, and as I consider it a work requiring careful preparation and constant advance, perhaps I may personally be as much profited in that as in any thing; and I may also be as useful."

"It is certainly a useful occupation," replied the pastor, "but to stand as a watchman on the walls of Zion, is an honor and a privilege far above price. It is not without its trials, but the servant of God must expect trials. I advise you to make it a subject of prayer, and if you decide upon the ministry, I will assist you in a collegiate and preparatory course. There is a fund for this purpose, which I am enabled partially to control, and which I can obtain for your benefit."

Walter thanked him, and promised to consider the matter. He felt grateful for the high regard his pastor had expressed for him, but he could not feel quite at liberty to accept the offer.

"Perhaps there is no better way for obtaining a finished education," said his mother. "A life spent in the ministry certainly can be useful."

"True," he replied, "but I do not feel sure that I have a call to the ministry. It would be wrong for me to accept these terms, unless I can fulfil the obligations they impose upon me. I do feel as though there was a work for me to do somewhere, but I cannot see what it is. I think I had better continue in my present course till light dawns upon me. We cannot find other duties by deserting the present ones which surround us;

but if we are faithful at our posts, our course will be made clear to us. I hope I am growing spiritually stronger every day."

"Well," replied Mrs. Martin, "you ought to be your own judge. It is not the college that makes the man, I know, and you must follow your own desires."

"I think, mother, that Providence will open a way for me to do whatever he has assigned as my portion in the life that now is."

He was strongly urged by others to prepare for a college course. It seemed to them that his natural abilities, and his devotion to study, both warranted and required that he should use the best advantages his country could bestow, whether he afterwards entered on the ministry or some other profession. But he replied:

"I believe I shall follow the guidance

of events, rather than attempt to fashion
them.   If there is a work for me to do,
my Father will make it manifest to me.
I am inclined to the belief that my
province is teaching.   To lead young
minds in the way of knowledge, to
guide young feet in the paths of virtue
and truth, not · forgetting to point them
to Jesus, is a great work, if truly followed."

Walter continued his studies this season with the same assiduity which had
characterized the previous years, growing in grace, and in the "nurture and
admonition of the Lord."   Greek was
now added to his other branches, and he
finally concluded to follow the counsel of
so many friends, and prepare for college.   Mr. Train was pleased with his
decision, and used his best efforts for his
advancement.

Early in the autumn he received a call

from his friends Mr. and Mrs. Childs,
who found him deeply absorbed in study,
and playfully reproached him for neglecting to visit them. Before leaving,
Mr. Childs said to him, "I have been
deputed by our district, unanimously, to
request you to teach our school again the
coming winter. And Mrs. Childs re-
quests your company in our family
again."

"I shall be very happy to accept both
offers," replied Walter. "I could not
please myself better in any situation."

"We are happy to hear you say so,"
said Mrs. Childs; "the children are
much attached to you, and we are pleased with your good influence over them."

After they were gone, Walter went to
his room, and knelt in thankfulness for
his many blessings, for kind and loving
friends, and for a heart to do God's will;
and then he prayed for guidance in his

vocation, and that he might be permitted
to lead the young minds of his charge to
a love for Jesus, and to a desire for use-
fulness in the world. A trusting serenity stole into his mind; and he felt
strengthened for a renewal of his labors,
by the assurance that the heavenly Shepherd was leading him gently up the steep
acclivities of life.

The autumn wore away, his school re-
commenced under prospering circumstances, and he applied himself with un-
usual assiduity, that he might sustain the
reputation he had previously won.

During this season a second blow fell
upon the mourning family of Mr. Martin.
Harry, prostrated by a falling tree in
the forests of the Saranac, was brought
home a lifeless form, to be laid beside his
brother Frank. The half-healed wound
of one year ago was opened afresh. The
mother became mute with intense grief,

and the remaining brothers seemed to say, as they gazed upon each other, "Which of us will be summoned next?"

How deep were the lessons which the young teacher garnered from these repeated blows of an unseen Providence. Life in this world, which might end at any moment, assumed a new importance. Every day given him seemed a treasure, a blank for him to fill with duties, which must be immediately performed, lest there come the relentless severing of the great messenger Death.

"Mother," said he, "our circle narrows, and we who are left must draw more closely around you, and support you with our love."

"We must endeavor to sustain her," he said to his brothers and sisters, "under these bereavements, as far as possible. What should we do without her? She is one of the best of mothers."

This was Walter's increasing sense of his duty. His father and his mother must be cherished and loved; and every day he was conscious of an increasing regard for their happiness.

His success in his school was equal to that in either of the preceding terms, and he now began to realize the substantial benefits of a well-earned reputation. He felt a security in his position, and continued for two years more in the same routine of studying and teaching. He improved steadily and surely, and now began to think seriously of entering college. He thought if he could obtain one or two terms of more advanced instruction than his own town afforded, his preparations would be quite satisfactory, for in mathematics he had gone beyond the requirements for entering a college course.

The last few months of the second year

brought additional changes in his loved home. The gay Herbert had yielded to the ravages of disease, and had gone to his rest, with a happy trust in his Saviour, and a sweet consciousness of his never-failing presence. It was almost difficult to mourn for one who seemed so joyful in the near presence of the happy land, and who left so sure a testimony of the blessedness of the Christian's trust.

Ere long Walter's brother Nat felt the weakness of disease stealing over him, and lest he too should fall a victim, he obtained his parents' ready consent that he should seek the far plains of Minnesota, if haply in that region of pure air he might regain his strength, and be spared a little longer. Ellen and Lizzie had gone to homes of their own choosing; so that Walter and his mother were left alone in their own home to sustain the sinking father, and keep alive the embers of the household fire. It was a great change for the ambitious young man, but a change which taught him patience, and developed a self-abandonment more noble than mere learning could give him.

"I had intended," said he to a friend who called upon him, "to have been away at school now; but I read to my mother such books as are interesting to her, and remain with her as much as possible, to comfort her, and assist her in the care of my father."

"It is a very sudden bereavement for your mother, and for you all, to lose so many in so brief a time," replied his friend; "and it seems but right that you should remain at home; but you must not despair. I am sorry to see your progress so suddenly interrupted."

"It is all for the best," replied Walter; "discipline will strengthen me, and I am sure I need strengthening."

A knock was heard at the door, and Walter admitted his valued friend Mr. Childs.

"Ah, my young friend," said the generous man, shaking him heartily by the hand, "how do you do to-day? I have come from home on purpose to see you. You are again in the deep waters of affliction, I hear."

"Yes, sir; our home has become very much changed. I alone am left to my mother, for my father is quite broken and helpless."

"I am sorry to hear it; very sorry. It breaks in upon your prospects and plans with a sudden chill. I hope you will not despond."

"No, sir, I think I do not. It hardly seems right to think of myself, in these bereavements of my father and mother.

One by one their children have departed, until they are almost like the branches of a leafless tree."

"Now no chastening for the present seemeth joyous, but grievous; nevertheless, afterwards it yieldeth the peaceable fruit of righteousness," said the kind man. "Come home with me, and stay a day or two. Mrs. Childs and Willie have sent an urgent request for you."

"Thank you," said Walter; "nothing could give me greater pleasure. But it would not be right for me to leave mother alone, even for a day. Father is so helpless, it is my duty to remain with her."

"Well," said Mr. Childs, "I never saw a cloud so dark but it broke away in time. The night may linger, but the dawn will surely come. Put your trust on high. Keep up your courage; and if

you can't come to me, I will come and
see you again ere long."

The cordial words of a friend so rich in
faith exerted a quickening influence over
Walter's energies, and he began gradually to look again for his books, and
to study by himself during the weeks
that followed; and soon the promised
dawn of the morning glimmered on the
horizon. A letter came from Lizzie, a
welcome letter, having every margin and
corner filled.

Lizzie wrote that her husband was
about to change his business, and that it
was her earnest desire to come back to
her own home. Her husband had expressed his willingness to come, and they
only awaited mother's consent.

"Mother," said Walter, "it is one of
God's providences. It is a golden drop
among us. Lizzie will be such a comfort
to you."

"It is indeed a blessing," said Mrs. Martin, "an unexpected blessing. Now you can be released and go to your school, without that anxious care for me which you otherwise would have had."

"I was not thinking of that, mother; I was thinking how happy you would be, how much Lizzie could do for you that I cannot do, and how the patter of little Eddie's feet would occupy your attention; and how beautifully you and father are provided for."

So the unselfish mother thought only of the happiness of her son, and the dutiful son considered the blessings which would accrue to his mother.

Preparations were immediately made for the reception of the loved ones, Walter interesting himself with his mother in all the domestic arrangements, until the glad day of the arrival came, bringing to the home a renewed animation and life.

"Mother," said Walter, coming into the house a few days after Lizzie's arrival, "I thought I could not leave you to teach this winter, and have refused all offers that would take me away; but to-day I have been requested to teach in our village, where I can board at home. How is it, Lizzie, do you want to board the schoolmaster this winter?"

"That depends upon who it is."

"Suppose it is the gentleman present?"

"I should be happy to keep him in the family," said she.

"Behold how the Lord provideth," added Mrs. Martin, for affliction had unsealed her lips, and she no longer hesitated to speak the thoughts of her heart. Affliction also had given Walter a faith he would never have learned in continued prosperity.

CHAPTER IX.

THE ENLISTMENT.

A WEEK of his school had passed away, and the interest he felt in his classes, and in the well-being of the young charge committed to his care, roused again his energies, and restored his natural impulse for books.

"I have got my school established," said he, "the classes are all in working order, and I must study evenings. I'll borrow a nook here by the side of your evening lamp, if you please, Lizzie, and try some more of those problems."

"Certainly," said she; "but I am afraid you will be a dull companion. I shall want to talk."

"If you must have a noise then," said

he, "suppose that I read to you, in something interesting. Here is a Life of Washington, and here is the best of all books, the Bible."

"Thank you," said she, "you can make your own selection, if you will only read something. When I have seen that father is comfortable, mother and I will be ready to listen."

"The programme for the evenings this winter," said Walter, "unless we are interrupted by callers, must be reading and study."

"I have been thinking," said Mrs. Martin, "that if I have Lizzie and the good son she has brought me, to help and care for me, and little Eddie to cheer me, you need not remain at home after your school closes. You can go to school if you wish, as you was intending to do last year.".

"I should like to go, mother, if you

think you will not be lonely without me. There is a club of young men forming to go from here. They are to board themselves, in order to reduce expenses, and I should like to join them. It is only twenty miles to the school by the railroad, so that I shall not be far away. I am sure that with a full course of preparatory study I can be more useful to the world, in some way, than without it. I have not yet visited Mr. Childs, as he requested me. I think I will go and take tea with him Saturday."

"I think you had better," said Mrs. Martin; "he is a kind friend and a good adviser."

Saturday soon came, and Walter found himself once more in the cheerful family circle of his hospitable friend. The children collected around him, and Mrs. Childs greeted him with her kindest welcome.

"I wish," said Willie, "you were teaching our school again this winter, as you used to."

"So do I," said Mr. Childs, "but he is needed at home. He is a great comfort there."

"I remember," said Willie, "when Jack·Dooley wanted to read a newspaper in school."

"Do you?" said Walter. "Jack did n't like me very well that day."

"No," said Willie; "but he liked you after that, and he likes you now better than any other teacher."

"I did not punish him."

"No ; you just looked him steadily in the eye till he yielded, and handed you the paper. But he was such a big, stout fellow, we were all frightened; for we thought you could not punish him, and that he would not obey unless he was punished."

"What do you suppose I was thinking, while I was looking at him?"

"I do n't know," said Willie; "what
were you?"

"At first I thought, 'You are a great,
strong boy, stronger than I am; if I attempt to punish you and you resist, I
shall get into trouble; if I give up without trying, my authority over you is
lost: and then I lifted my heart to God
for guidance and assistance in the hour
of my helplessness, and help came. Jack
and I became the best of friends after
that."

"I know it," said Willie; "I could
not understand that at all."

"I will tell you," said Walter. "I
watched my opportunity, and had some
private talks with him. I spoke to his
heart; told him for what life was given
us; spoke of Jesus, of our need of salvation through his name, of the eternal fu-

ture, and what is required of us in this present life. Your father has told you all these things from your infancy, Willie; but Jack had known very little of them."

"Perhaps that is what has improved him so much," said Willie; "he is quite a different boy from what he used to be."

"I think Willie and I must become his friends," said Mr. Childs, "if that is the case. I have always regarded him as a kind of vagabond, who could n't be improved."

"You could n't do a greater deed of charity than to help him along a little," replied Walter.

"We never had a teacher that won the hearts of the children as you did," observed Mrs. Childs.

"Perhaps you never had one who tried as much to win them," replied

Walter. "The hearts of the children was what I wanted. Then I was sure of success, and possessed the key by which I could wind and unwind them at my pleasure. I always aimed to teach them self-respect, and praised them when there was a chance for it. There is no use in constantly chiding children, and depreciating their efforts. When they have really tried to do right, the teacher should commend them. We all like to be praised, and children are but miniature men and women. They should be interested too in something aside from their regular lessons. They get tired of dull monotony."

After some more pleasant conversation about school matters, Mr. Childs asked Walter, "What shall you do when your present term closes?"

"I think, sir, that I shall join a club of young men who are going to the old standing academy twenty miles above here, at Fairdale."

"That is a good plan. Do so, by all means. If Willie was old enough, I would send him with you. I hope you will be in college ere long."

"Thank you, sir," said Walter, "for your kind wishes. I also hope I may be."

Walter's visit was a great benefit to his depressed spirits, invigorating him for renewed exertions, and restoring in a measure his wonted energies. His term of teaching glided swiftly to its close, and a few weeks afterwards he was busily at work in the academy. Several of the young men of the club were his acquaintances, the others soon formed intimacies, and they became a very harmonious club.

The academy had been long established, was admirably provided with teachers, and Walter found himself advancing rapidly. He continued there through the season, with the exception of the summer vacation, which he improved by remaining at home and gladdening the heart of his mother. Her happiness was his highest wish, her comfort his constant care. The increasing feebleness of his father caused a double anxiety, lest his mother too should be prostrated by sorrow and care.

"Let me do all I can for you," he would say to her. "It belongs to me now to be your burden-bearer. God has laid it upon me, and I have no desire to do otherwise."

Ah, how little does man know his own heart, or understand his own future! Young men living in ease and serenity, and looking forward with high hopes to the future; and old men boasting of their country, and trusting in its great strength:

such were the men of our nation in the autumn before the terrible rebellion broke out, which made such sudden and fearful changes.

When Walter assumed to be the burden-bearer of his mother, he had no premonition that another work would claim his attention, or that he possibly could consider another duty paramount to the one now so high in his estimation.

Through the presidential campaign he had watched with great interest the progress of the public mind; laughing with others at the threats of secession, and believing they were mere bravado. When the voting time came, he went home with all the eagerness of patriotic youth to exercise the great prerogative of freemen at the ballot-box. He cast in his vote, and returned immediately to school.

But ere long the storm burst forth. The war-cloud gathered blackness, and

spread over a larger and still larger ter-
ritory. The whole country was aroused
and alarmed, and when government called for an army of seventy-five thousand
men, to sustain and enforce its authority,
a new sense awoke in millions of minds
that we had something to defend that
was worth all the sacrifices it might require, however great.

Walter watched, and listened, and
thought. Mother, books, every thing
but country lost their wonted ascendency
in his heart. "What do I here?" said
he. "Why do I wait? Is my blood
better than the blood of my compatriots,
that I should guard it with a jealous
care? Books! education! of what avail
is all that to me, with a country shatter-
ed and ruined by treason?" He piled
away his books, and took the cars for
home.

"My son," said the startled mother,

"what has brought you home so soon? You must be ill."

"Why, mother, this horrid war. It is not right that I should be at school. Our country needs me; will you let me go?"

It was a most trying question. What wonder that the oft-bereaved mother replied,

"Walter, it is true our country needs men; but there are so many ready to go, that I cannot think you are needed. No, I cannot spare you. I have hoped so much from you. You are all I have of my long line of boys."

"I know it, mother, I know 't is very hard; but if our country is not saved, you do not want a son. I am well and strong. I look at my arms, my feet, and my hands, and I see they are as well fitted for duty as other men's. I am ashamed to walk the streets and see my friends who have enlisted, and I yet lingering here."

But when he saw how unconvinced and distressed she was, his conscience smote him. He thought perhaps his duty was at home; it could not lie in two directions at the same time. Then he saw his father, nervous and pale, and decided to postpone enlisting, for the present at least.

He went into the shed, and finding there a quantity of wood not yet sawed, he said to himself, "Now that I am here, I will stay at home two or three days, and saw and pile this wood. It will seem natural to mother to have me around at work, and compensate perhaps for the anxiety I have caused her; besides, the exercise will be beneficial to my health. Then I will go back to school."

The mother was comforted, and Wal-

ter sawed on, sometimes cheerfully, sometimes dreamily pausing over the work as
he thought of his country.

Two days passed away, and he had
become quite calm, when he went out
into the village to call upon some friends
and get the papers.

Everybody was excited, the papers
were full of enthusiasm, and a large company was already formed in the town.
"Only for three months," said they.
"Come, Walter, join us. It is the duty
of every man. Watson will be our captain, and he is the very best man in the
town."

Walter knew that was true. A better
man could not be found, and some of the
first young men in the village had already enlisted. He returned home with
his ardor kindled anew, read the stirring
news in the papers, and went to his bed,
but not to sleep. The fire burned within

him. "Mother and Lizzie are certainly mistaken," he said; "they do not understand the country's peril. My duty towards my mother is to fight for her and her home."

He had decided; and when breakfast was over, he said, "Mother, I am going out to put my name under Captain Watson."

She looked at him calmly, and replied, "I have said all that I can, Walter. Go, if you feel that you must."

He accepted her answer, and went out. An hour after, he returned; the deed was done. He had enlisted.

CHAPTER X.

THE CAMP.

WE have seen Walter in the factory, a steadfast witness for Jesus; we have seen him in school, training young minds to virtue and true self-respect; we have had a glimpse of him in the filial duties of home; and we turn to him now in the camp.

Mrs. Martin gave him no word of reproach; she knew it was a sense of duty that had taken him from her. She asked when the company would leave town, and he replied, "In three days." Silently she went about the necessary preparations. Not a murmur, not a censure escaped her; but the compressed lips and downcast eyes spoke the struggles of the heart more plainly than words, and her silent manner was more dreadful to Walter than open rebuke. He doubted more and more whether he had done right, and was tortured between the two ideas, the grief of his parents and the calls of his country. In imagination he saw his mother droop and die, and he trembled lest he should indeed be the cause of such an event. He found no rest from these thoughts day or night.

But if his mother did not reproach him, Lizzie did. She told him plainly that he had done wrong, and that the mother's silent agony was more alarming than noisy grief. But what could be done? There stood his name written with his own hand, and he could not retract.

Captain Watson himself called to see Mrs. Martin. He represented to her the great need of patriotism, reminded her that it was but for three months they enlisted, told her how much he respected Walter, and how much the army would need the influence of young men like him—that he undoubtedly would rise to the officers' ranks; and finally requested her to become the 'comforter of his own wife and two little girls, whom he must confide to the care of friends left behind.

This call was appreciated by the bereaved mother, who especially rested on the idea of the short term of enlistment, and whose thoughts also went out to the bereaved wife and children of the captain, and to the numerous other mothers parting like herself from loved sons.

Three busy, anxious days sped over the village, then the company assembled with music and a flag, and called at the captain's door, where they found a collation provided for them; after which, marching through the streets, they bade farewell to the scenes of home and all

they loved on earth. To Mrs. Martin
the martial music was like a funeral
knell, though troops of boys threw up
their caps and seemed to think it far
otherwise.

When twilight shadowed the green
vales, captain and men were far away,
and praying hearts at home were
breathing forth the earnest cry to God
that he would guard them and save
them.

The morning sun shone upon Walter
in a new situation. The camp where the
regiment was to await the uniforms provided by the state, consisted of tents
hastily arranged, where the new compa-
nies congregated as they arrived. What
a bustle! what a confusion! Walter half
opened his eyes, bewildered by the unaccustomed situation, when the beat of the
morning drum brought him to immedi-
ate consciousness. He bounded to his

feet in an instant, while a new thrill of patriotism ran through his veins.

"Halloo here!" said he, shaking up a drowsy companion; "on duty, sir. Do n't you hear the 'roll of the drum, and the trumpet that speaks of fame?'"

As his comrades aroused themselves and began to converse, a shocking oath greeted his ear, and he started as though stung by some venomous insect. He looked around for some secret place for morning devotions, but there was no retirement there; so breathing a silent prayer, he entered upon the duties of the day. He liked the drill and the military parade, and felt the great throbbings of a new manhood within him, a more earnest desire to serve his country, and a willingness to give his life for her cause.

"What do you think of camp life?" asked Captain Watson a few days after.

"I should like it pretty well," replied Walter, "if I had a few more congenial companions. The men are pretty rough, more so than I imagined they would be."

"Yes," replied the captain, "they feel unrestrained, and some whom I thought pretty fair young men at home, seem rather wild here; but they will grow sober again; they are made of good material, and will be great fighters. You must consider that your standard of moral character is high."

"They seem very little prepared to fall in battle," said Walter.

"Very true," replied the captain; "but we have got an excellent chaplain appointed for us, and I hope much from his influence."

When a week had passed away, Walter found himself quite at home in his new position. Two of his old factory companions, Tom Hardy and Ned Man-

son, were in his company; and here too
he found Jack Dooley, his refractory
scholar; and he was rejoiced to see what
excellent young men they had become.
Tom was an earnest Christian, and became a fellow-laborer with Walter in
seeking the best interests of the men.

The Christian, if true to his heavenly
calling, can readily be distinguished in a
company of the thoughtless; and though,
in the sunshine of prosperity, they may
laugh at him, he becomes their refuge in
times of trouble and sorrow. So Walter
soon found himself the great reliance of
many of the young soldiers when per-
plexed by difficulties.

"Why don't you smoke, corporal?"
said a young man to Walter, who had
just been appointed to that station.

"I never had a fancy for it," replied
Walter.

"You must learn now then," replied

the soldier; "when a fellow is away from home so, a good cigar is a real comfort."

"It would be a discomfort to me," said Walter; "besides, I think it is a bad habit, and should not be willing to try it. It would be better for you to leave it off. It would be better for your pocket, and better for your morals."

"Ho, my morals are well enough. I do n't drink; and only take a cigar now and then."

"It may lead to other things which are bad," replied Walter. "Suppose you try to break the habit. I find no necessity for it, and it will increase upon you perhaps. Take the money and buy books, they will be better than cigars when you are lonely."

"Perhaps you are right," replied the young man; "I should like some books, that's a fact. I believe I'll try that

plan. My mother and sisters were always opposed to my smoking."

"Well," said Walter, "write to them your new resolution; and they will be so pleased you will not regret the self-denial."

The change of diet, though acceptable to Walter, was not relished by many of the men, who were fresh from the bountiful tables of their homes.

"The beef grows tougher and the bread harder every day," one of the men said at dinner one day. "I say, we can't stand this. If Uncle Sam employs us, he must give us better living than this."

"They've got good beef here," said another, "I know; I've seen it, and we ought to have it."

Some oaths were uttered that seemed terrible to Walter's ears, though he had been hearing profanity every day of his camp life.

"Do n't swear," said he, "do n't swear, and I'll get some better beef for you to-morrow. When we get down among the rebels, I suppose we must eat such as we can get; but it seems hard here. We have n't got toughened yet. But if you wont swear, I'll get some beef for you to-morrow."

"Well, produce the beef," said one, "and I wont swear again for a week."

After dinner he went out to find the man who dealt out the beef.

"Sir," said he, stepping up to him quickly and assuming a stern countenance, "sir, have n't you any better beef than that we had to-day? It was n't fit for the dogs to eat."

The old man looked up at him with astonishment. He was surprised at the indignant flash of Walter's eyes.

"Why, corporal," said he, "are you angry? I thought you was a Christian."

"So I am," replied Walter; "but I am a civilized Christian, and I cannot eat such beef as that was. It would raise the indignation of any Christian to see men trying to eat such a dinner as our men tried to eat to-day. If it is n't better to-morrow, I shall report you to higher authority."

The next day the beef was good, and the men were warm in their thanks.

"I do not want any thanks," said Walter; "only keep your promise, and not swear."

It was pretty hard for unrestrained men to keep such a promise as that; but they tried so earnestly, that there was much less profanity in their tent; for when the promised week was ended, none seemed ready to fall back to their old habits.

But tobacco and profanity were not so destructive as the arch-enemy intemperance. Whiskey was a more formidable opponent than any other which Walter had to encounter.

It was fearful to the young Christian to see men around him deprived of their reason, brutal and insensible through the influence of this terrible scourge. He saw too that some of the officers were no better than the men, and wondered how they were to guide their men when they could not guide themselves.

"I think," said Captain Watson, "it would be well to try some prayer-meetings. You could find a few who would help sustain one, could you not?"

"I think I could," replied Walter. "There are Tom Hardy, Pardee, Jones, and some others. I am glad I have your permission. I will appoint one for to-night."

Walter entered upon the work in earnest, and many were induced to attend the "corporal's prayer-meeting," as they called it, because "the corporal was an honorable, kind, first-rate fellow;" and they "would go to his prayer-meeting, if they never went to another."

"I tell you," said Ben Brown, "the corporal is n't one of your mean kind of Christians. He do n't talk to you about your soul, and then, when you ask him a favor, put on a long face and say he can't grant it."

"That's a fact," replied Johnson; "if he sees a fellow in trouble, he puts his hand in his pocket and pulls out his last cent for him. And if one of us is sick, he is always ready; and if anybody is abused, he is sure to defend them. Three cheers for the corporal's religion and the corporal's prayer-meeting. I'm going to hear him pray."

The little seed thus sown by Walter and his friends was not scattered in vain.

It not only bore good fruit in the hearts of some of the men; so that the still small voice of contrition was heard, and the sounds of wickedness were exchanged for the songs of praise, but the prayer-meetings became permanent, and their influence caused religion to strike deeper root in the mind of Walter. Every day he saw more and more the value of a trust in Jesus. He saw also how much the soldiers needed a true friend and counsellor, and his affections grew increasingly interested in their welfare. Many of them were young, brought up under the guidance of loving parents, never before thrown upon their own resources, and it was not surprising if they went astray, needing both temporal and spiritual help.

"Oh, Walter," said Robert Fay, who had been one of Walter's schoolmates under Mr. Train, "I do n't know what I shall do. I have n't got a cent of money left. You know I had leave of absence yesterday, and went off to have a good time, and spent all I had. I did n't mean to, but the boys went in for a supper and a treat, and I did n't want to be mean, so I have n't any thing left."

"Do you need some money?" asked Walter.

"Yes, I do need some; but I have not any way to get it, unless I can sell my guitar. I never shall use it any more. I do n't want to carry it south with me, and I suppose we shall go in a few days."

"What do you ask for the guitar?"

"I would sell it for two dollars, but I do n't know of anybody that would buy it."

"I'll buy it," said Walter, "and send it to my little nieces. But, Robert, how much better it would be for you if you

would not go with such men. I am afraid
they will lead you into worse trouble
than losing your money; I am afraid you
will lose your soul."

Robert dropped his head, and was
silent. Walter continued,

"You are a soldier for your country,
Robert; be a soldier for Jesus. Come
to our prayer-meeting to-night."

Robert consented, and afterwards the
prayer-meeting became his greatest pleasure. Thus another was won by Walter's
method of reaching the soul, through first
relieving the wants of the body.

Was not Walter right? Was not this
the method of our Saviour? Did he not
heal the body, and then say, "Thy sins
are forgiven thee?" Did he not feed the
multitude, sending them away full and
happy, instead of faint and weary? So
Walter turned not scornfully away from
the wicked in the camp, but became to

them the ready sympathizer and the kind friend, thus gaining the ascendency of love over them, by which he won them to Christ.

But now there came another call over the country. Three hundred thousand men were wanted "for three years or the war." More homes must be entered, and more hearts desolated. Many who left home for three months only, now signed their names for three years. But Walter refused.

"I would almost as willingly stand up before the enemy and be shot," he wrote to Ellen, "as refuse to enlist for the war. It seems cowardly. But I have promised mother, and I must keep my promise. I know that she is living on the hope that I will soon be at home."

"I am sorry," said Captain Watson, "that you do not go south with us. Your influence is invaluable. The officers all want you. You can have a commission if you will go."

"Thank you, sir," replied Walter; "I should certainly go if it was not for my mother. She cannot be persuaded to give her consent, and I do not feel justified in going without it. My father is very feeble, more so than ever."

The next day some of the higher officers of the regiment spoke to Walter in flattering terms, and offered to procure him a commission if he would go; but he felt that his promise to his mother was a sacred thing, and no inducements could persuade him to break it. He assisted in the breaking up of the camp, bade farewell to the comrades who loved him, and though his thoughts and his wishes followed them, he returned to his home to comfort his parents, and again resume the every-day duties of private life.

CHAPTER XI.

THE MISSION.

"Oh my son," said Mrs. Martin, as she once more grasped his hand, and felt his warm kiss upon her cheek, "I am so thankful to see you at home once more."

"I am glad to be here, mother," he replied; "but it seems wrong to seek the comforts of home, when so many brave men are going forth to battle for our country's good. I feel that it is mean and unworthy to shirk my duty thus."

"You must remember," said Lizzie, "that you do not shirk. It is not that. You only leave one duty that you may fulfil another. It is perhaps as much a duty to attend to mother and to father, under the circumstances, as to fight for your country, though it may not flatter your patriotism quite so much."

"I think I realize all my duties to them," replied Walter; "but other parents yield up their sons; they give them freely for their country."

"Very true," replied Lizzie; "but you must reflect that our parents have just passed through a series of severe trials; and that father is almost helpless, and cannot remain with us long."

"I know it, sister, and I am ready to fulfil my duties here. I will not leave mother again."

"I do not ask that," said Mrs. Martin. "I do not require that you remain with me all the time. I know your best interests demand that you should be away, nor would I withhold you from your country in her need; but I ask you to reflect whether there are not other ways in which you can serve her as truly as in the army's ranks."

"Perhaps so," replied Walter; "but it appears to me that just now our nation needs plenty of powder and ball, and men to use them. I have become deeply impressed too with the religious wants of the army, and I should like to remain with those young men to sympathize with them and lead them to Jesus. But if duty keeps me at home, all honor to the brave men who are gone, and to those who may go. And now let us drop the subject, for since I have come home to make you happy, I must think about my employment here. Did you send for my books?"

"Yes," replied Mrs. Martin, "they are all at home."

"Then I can study some," said he. "To-morrow I think I will go out and see Mr. Childs."

That evening Walter went to the post-office, and received many cordial greetings from the people who crowded around him with inquiries for their loved ones in camp. Occasionally the questions, "What did you back out for?" and, "Why did n't you go ahead with the others?" tinged his cheeks with crimson, for he was sensitive on this point, and could not brook that his filial obedience should be misconstrued into cowardice or recreancy.

He was somewhat humbled by the implied taunts; but, conscious that he had endeavored to act in conformity with his sense of right, he felt that those who did not understand his motives and situation had no right to judge his conduct.

"Surely," he thought, as he walked slowly home, "God will direct me in the way I should go, if I but lean upon his arm. I will wait patiently, and he shall direct my steps."

The next day he took the familiar road to the home of Mr. Childs, and was greeted with the cordial welcome of previous days.

"Really," said the good pastor, "you have taken a new color, if you have n't been far south. You are quite brown, a good, healthy color."

"Yes, sir," said Walter, smiling; "being in the wind and fresh air so much is an excellent thing for the complexion. It takes out the milk and water, and gives the fresh, ruddy bloom of health."

"Is n't it fun," asked Willie, "to live as they do in camp?"

"It is not exactly fun," said Walter, "it is rather too hard for that; but it is pretty exhilarating sometimes. It is exciting business for us quiet people to be learning how to shoot our fellow-men.

Camp life may do very well here, but there will be hardships enough when they reach the scene of action."

"I wish I was a little older," said Willie with kindling eye, "I should try it pretty quick. How wicked for those rebels to attempt to dissolve our Union."

"Yes," said Walter, "that is the idea which sustains the soldiers in the prospect before them. They talk these things over, and become more patriotic every day. There will be a large missionary field in the army," continued he, addressing Mr. Childs. "It is surprising how soon young men who have been well trained at home, catch the new habits about them; and in camp men of all kinds are thrown promiscuously together."

"This war will open to us many new duties," replied Mr. Childs. "Have you formed any plans yet for yourself?"

"Nothing definite," said Walter. "I

cannot feel quite like entering college in times like these. When men are nerving for the fight, and blood is being freely offered, and clouds are thick and black, I cannot sit down tamely to a four years' study of Greek and Latin. I ought not so to use my time. I ought to be at work, helping my countrymen in some way."

"You are enthusiastic," said Mr. Childs; "you savor of the camp, but I believe you are right. We must be enthusiastic, or our country will fail. And yet," he added thoughtfully, "it is rather anomalous for me, whose business it is to teach men the way of peace, to say to them, 'You must fight.'"

"This seems home-like," said Walter, as he took his accustomed seat at the table. "You see, Mrs. Childs, I have been dining lately from a tin plate and eating soup from a tin cup."

Ada laughed merrily. "I should like to see that way of dining," said she.

"I should like to try it," said Willie.

"Well, I am glad you are not old enough," said Ada. "Do you think, Mr. Martin, that it is right for all the boys and men to be so eager to go off to fight and die?"

"Yes," said Walter, "I think they ought to be willing to give themselves in a cause so just as ours; but I admit it is a great sacrifice for the mothers and sisters who remain at home."

"I should like to go," said Willie. "I should like to stand face to face with the ugliest regiment this side of the Gulf."

"You hardly realize what you say, Willie," said Mr. Childs. "War is a solemn thing. It is not to be desired or sought, and must be accepted only when every alternative fails."

Walter enjoyed every moment of his

visit, and at night when he parted from the beloved minister and received his best wishes, he felt stronger in that hopeful confidence in Christ which is "an anchor to the soul, both sure and steadfast." He determined anew that each day he would seek for strength to perform the duties of that day, leaving the result with Him whose promise is for ever sure.

Some weeks passed away, during which he remained to bless his mother with his loving presence, taking unwearied care of his invalid father, striving to forget his own desires, and growing firmer in the faith that if his heavenly Master had a work for him to do, He would make it known to him in due time; and having committed himself to the great, loving Shepherd, he knew that he was safe in his care.

The morning rays of a pleasant day shone upon the pale face of Mrs. Martin

as she stood at her window watching the
steps of her only son returning from his
accustomed walk to the post-office; and
as she noted his firm and manly mien,
she said to herself, "I have no boys now,
the last one is already a man. I must
yield him up to the stage of action; I
cannot expect him to live this indolent
life and be happy."

"Mother," said he, coming briskly in,
"I have a letter from Mr. Eastman."

"What does he write?" she asked.

"He says that he is about to give up
the academy he is teaching, to prepare
for the ministry; and that he will rec-
ommend me to the trustees if I wish it.
Do you think I had better accept the
offer?"

Mrs. Martin considered a moment, and
then said, "The hand of the Lord is in
it, Walter. You need some employment; my wants are supplied, and I am

happy with Lizzie. You like teaching, and I must not ask you to live in idleness. You are safe from danger there."

Walter smiled. "I am safe anywhere, mother, under the protection of Him who ever watcheth us."

"I know it, my son; but I can not shake off this terrible fear of losing you."

The young man thought of the three mounds yet fresh with the dews of weeping, of the two sons away on the far wild prairie, of the invalid husband and father, and he could find no words of reproach for the lacerated heart of the loving mother. He next mentioned the offer to his father, and asked him if he thought he could spare him.

"I suppose it is best that you should go," replied Mr. Martin; "but you will see me no more in this world."

"Oh father," replied Walter, "I hope I shall; I hope you will live a long time yet, though you may not be well again as you used to be."

"No," said Mr. Martin, "it cannot be; I feel that I shall go soon."

The result proved the truth of the father's anticipations : erelong Walter was called from his school to see another added to the list of those already gone beyond this vale. As he went about the desolate house, and memory recalled the jovial voices and the familiar countenances of those who so lately had occupied those rooms, he asked himself why he was spared.

"Why is the full tide of health flushing through my veins?" he said. "Am I better than they? Nay, verily; and if I am still kept on the earth, it is because there is a work for me to do. Heavenly Father, teach me what that work is, and grant me grace for its performance."

A still small voice within replied, "Do

thy duty this day. The morrow's work shall be told thee when the morrow comes."

"This is all I need to know," said he. "This day my duty is towards my mother; I'll seek her now."

He found her sitting dreamily in the next room, and taking a chair by her side he softly placed his arm about her neck.

"Mother," said he, "the house is silent and voiceless. I cannot leave you here. Lizzie has her husband and little one to comfort her; why cannot you go and stay with Ellen till the first sadness is worn off? I suppose I must return to my school."

"My son," said she, "the sadness rests too heavily to be easily worn away anywhere; but I will do as you think best."

Ellen welcomed the stricken mother

with her whole affections, and Walter returned to his school.

Meantime the battle's tramp, the deathly struggles, and the soldiers' groans were ringing from hill to hill; the cries for more help came up from our armies in the field, and Walter could with difficulty suppress the burning desire to go forth for his beloved country and her suffering cause. Every evening was occupied with the news from the scene of conflict, and the soul of the young man kindled with longings to participate in the active labors of the fearful work.

He thought of the young men, pale with wounds and agony; of their wearisome marches and nights of watching; of the unprepared souls passing away to the eternal Judge, and he longed to be there to comfort and to heal, and to point the perishing to Jesus, "who taketh away the sin of the world."

God, who had put these desires within him, opened a way by which he could fulfil the wishes of his daily thoughts. The young pastor of the village called upon him, and as they conversed upon the theme current in every mouth, Walter opened his heart and frankly expressed his inmost wishes.

"I cannot rest contented here," he said, "my country needs me; and yet my mother is so unwilling that I should enter the army, that I am unable to decide where my duty lies."

"Perhaps I can make a suggestion," said Mr. Carnes, "which will be a compromise. Go as a missionary in the army. Perhaps your mother will consent to that; and you may be as useful as if you should take the musket and enter the field."

The idea was pleasing to Walter's ardent mind, but he could see no way for the accomplishment of such a purpose.

"I can assist you," said Mr. Carnes, "and get you an appointment."

Walter agreed to this immediately, provided he could obtain his mother's consent. He found this an easier task than he expected; and at the close of his term he left the quiet north, to seek her brave men who were giving themselves on the altar of freedom, in the sanguinary conflict, in weariness and in perils.

"If I may but lead the lost to Jesus," he said, "I would willingly share their sufferings and bear their toil."

In a letter to his mother he wrote, "If you could see the joy with which the men welcome me, mother, you would rejoice that you had the opportunity of giving me to this cause. I am glad I am here. I only ask the high privilege of laboring for my fellow-men. I think of you, dear mother, and you will pray for me, and our Father will hear your prayers. Should I ever teach again, as I formerly thought God designed me to do, I should like to teach in these southern lands, until ignorance and sin are dispelled from her borders, and freedom waves her flag over the hearts of her sons."

CHAPTER XII.

WALTER'S CONCLUSION.

THE closing words of Walter's letter
indicate the new ideas which were dawn-
ing upon him. He saw a new field for
teaching. A new sphere of labor opened before him, and he thought the early
and repeated callings which had been in
his heart from the, time he left the factory till now, callings to prepare for a
life of teaching, which had haunted him
even while infatuated for the army, were
about to be realized. His heavenly Father had directed his steps to the land
of the benighted, where the harvest was
plenteous.

Walking over the dusty roads of Vir-
ginia one warm day, he paused to remove
his hat and wipe the perspiration from

his brow, when an aged man of a dark hue rose from the ground and saluted him.

"Ah, my friend," said Walter, "this is a warm day. But what have you there in your hand?"

"Dis, massa, is a hymn-book I'se been readin'."

"Can you read?" asked Walter.

"Yes, massa, I larn to read when I was a boy, toting ole massa's chil'ern to school. They teach me how to read. Ole massa was awful mad, an' he whip me 'cause I know how; but I say, 'Whip on, ole feller; you can't whip dat out of me, no way."

"And what do you think of the times now?" asked Walter.

"'Pears like dey mighty good, massa. Ole massa leave me, Massa Lincoln make me free; de Union people give me dis hymn-book, an' dis yer," drawing a

Bible from his pocket; "an' bress de Lord, I can read 'em an' nobody to whip me."

Walter found these colored people wherever he went. Men and women, boys and girls appeared before him at every turn, and his heart warmed with pity for them. There were not many who could read like the old man by the road-side; they were ignorant, and every day the conviction gained a hold upon Walter's mind that instruction was the life-work to which he was called.

"I never could understand my mission at the North," said he, "and now I see the reason. My work was not there. Here the fields are white for the harvest; already other laborers are putting in the sickle and gathering the full grain; I must join their band, and thrust my sickle in with theirs."

The wish of his heart has been gratified, and every day he gathers the dark faces about him and instructs them as he formerly instructed the pale-faced children of the North.

"When I go to school in the morning," he says, "they meet me and eagerly tell me how much they have learned since yesterday; and I endeavor to put in their hearts the true ideas of manhood. I have in my school nearly a dozen George Washingtons; for the poor mothers, having no name of their own, delight in bestowing the names of great men upon their children.

"Every day their black faces glisten upon me as I teach them; they sing to me the songs of Jesus, and I am contented with the mission my God has given me. What the future may bring forth is hidden with my Father; but I know that they who put their trust in Him shall surely prosper. With the wise preacher I can say, 'Let us hear the conclusion of the whole matter: Fear God, and keep his commandments; for this is the whole duty of man.'"